KATHERINE KARLIN

SEND ME WORK

Stories

TriQuarterly Books
Northwestern University Press
Evanston, Illinois

TriQuarterly Books
Northwestern University Press
www.nupress.northwestern.edu

Printed in the United States of America

10 9 8 7 6 5 4 3 2 1

Library of Congress Cataloging-in-Publication Data

Karlin, Katherine.
    Send me work : stories / Katherine Karlin.
        p. cm.
    Short stories, some previously published.
    ISBN 978-0-8101-5220-5 (pbk. : alk. paper)
    I. Title.
PS3611.A7838S46 2011
813.6—dc22

                                                    2011014683

∞ The paper used in this publication meets the minimum requirements of the
American National Standard for Information Sciences—Permanence of Paper
for Printed Library Materials, ANSI Z39.48-1992.

For Chris Remple

Contents

Acknowledgments

I wish to thank the people at Northwestern University Press: Mike Levine, Elizabeth Levenson, and Marianne Jankowski. I am deeply indebted to my agent, Barbara Braun.

I would also like to thank the many magazine and journal editors who selected these stories for publication: Hannah Tinti, Howard Junker, Mathew Timmons, Andrew Tonkovich, Ronald Spatz, Tom Christie, Gina Frangello, Tatyana Mishel, Joseph Levens, and Paula Closson Buck. Thank you Bill Henderson, Kathy Pories, and Madison Smartt Bell. To Amaranth Borsuk and Bryan Hurt, the curators of the Loudest Voice Reading Series in Los Angeles, where many of these stories got their start, my love and gratitude.

"Bye-Bye, Larry" first appeared in ZYZZYVA 21, no. 1 (Spring 2005): 49–61, and also appeared in *The Pushcart Prize XXXI*, ed. Bill Henderson (Wainscott, N.Y.: Pushcart Press, 2007), 245–56.

"The Severac Sound" appeared in *Other Voices* 44 (Summer 2006): 187–202.

"Muscle Memory" appeared in *One Story*, no. 103, and also *New Stories from the South*, ed. Kathy Pories and Madison Smartt Bell (Chapel Hill: Algonquin Books, 2009), 1–23.

"Send Me Work" appeared in *In Posse Review* (October 2008), http://www.inpossereview.com.

"Staggered Maturities" appeared in *Joyland* (June 2009), http://www.joylandmagazine.com, *CellStories* (November 13, 2009), and *The Loudest Voice* 1 (2010): 75–78.

"Stand Up, Scout" appeared in *The Summerset Review* 2 (2008) and *The Best of Summerset Review* 2 (2008), 117–30.

"The Good Word" appeared in the *LA Weekly Literary Supplement* 29, no. 26 (May 18, 2007).

"Underwater" appeared in *Santa Monica Review* 22, no. 2 (2010): 81–92.

"Seven Reasons" appeared in *Alaska Quarterly Review* 25, nos. 1 and 2 (Fall/Winter 2008): 208–16.

"Geography" appeared in *West Branch* 68 (Spring/Summer 2011): 14–31.

SEND ME
WORK

BYE-BYE, LARRY

Larry Michalik did not die a glorious refinery death. He did not explode in a fireball as the spark of a welder's torch ignited methane fumes. He was not sheared by the claws of railcars coupling in the yard. He did not dive into the mouth of a flare stack, leaving behind his work boots on the diamond-plate catwalk. He did not wander into an empty tank, purged with nitrogen, and drown in the oxygen-free air. Larry Michalik merely lowered his union coffee mug one morning, dropped his head, and went out like a flame. We thought he had dozed off. For the rest of the shift we prodded him with the eraser end of a pencil, jotted down his readings, and silenced the alarms buzzing on his control board. Only when Larry's relief showed up did we realize he was dead.

Here's where I should eulogize Larry. For the most part, oil men are easy to like. When I started this job they all looked the same to me, but I make a point of drawing from each a story. On the evening shift, in spring, when the refinery lights twinkle against the darkening sky and we fish plastic bottles out of the sludge pond, I get them to reveal something personal. One keeps a girlfriend and a whole secret family in Florida. Another committed acts of sabotage before the '83 strike. A third has a brother serving time. You never know what a man will tell a young woman, warm and receptive, who is not his wife. I don't care if the stories are true; the moment is full and tender. Days later I will pass the same man on the hot tarmac or in the bright light of the control room and electricity crackles in the air between us. We don't even have to look at each other.

But strip away Larry Michalik's blandness and there was more blandness. The closest thing he had to a hobby was Ann-Margret. He taped in his locker a life-size poster of young Ann-Margret in a minidress and go-go boots, her chin tucked coquettishly and her hair blown into an after-sex tangle.

"I tell you what, Gina," Larry said to me once. "She looks better at sixty than you do in your twenties. Better than you ever will."

I dug my fists into the pockets of my coveralls. "I like the movie she made with Bette Davis," I said. "You know. The one where Bette Davis is a drunk old beggar woman and Ann-Margret's her daughter being raised in a convent overseas, who thinks her mother is some fancy society lady. Then Ann-Margret brings home her fiancé, who's, like, the prince of Spain, and Bette Davis has to get Glenn Ford to help her clean up and pretend she's rich." My voice cranked up a notch with excitement. "Right up to the end of the movie you expect her to admit that she's just an old drunk, so the daughter can tell her she loves her for who she is. But what's cool is that Bette Davis pulls it off. It's the only movie I ever saw that says lying is the best policy."

I watched Larry's face for a sign of recognition. He just looked into the distance and said, "She was just a young filly in that one. What a beautiful girl."

The fact is, I just didn't care much for the deceased.

Before the wake we stumble off the midnight shift and gather at Stan's taproom. The wives will meet us at the widow's house, bringing tuna casseroles and Jell-O molds. Stan's is nothing more than a room with a long counter and a single neon Rolling Rock ad and a mirror so corroded it reflects nothing. I sip a beer and roll cork coasters down the length of the bar; dressed in my girl clothes, a denim jacket frayed at the collar and a short denim skirt, I feel bare.

Franny Sadlowski and Chessie Cesare sit on the next bar stools. Chessie, our shop steward, has the *Philadelphia Inquirer* open to the business page. Franny reads aloud a quiz from a copy of his girlfriend's *Cosmopolitan* called "Are You *Truly* Honest with Him?"

Here's what I know about Franny. He has a round little potbelly like a piglet. He's thirty-nine and his girlfriend is seventeen.

About Chessie I know this: he's forty-three and has a long, sad Sicilian face. After his divorce he moved in with a real estate agent, ten years his senior. In the mornings he takes his coffee and newspaper out on the balcony of their condo and props his feet on the railing, and he watches his real estate agent go off to work in her mint-colored suit, her hair a shimmery blond helmet, joining the other attractive divorcées who stream out of the building every morning—a river of travel agents, executive assistants, event planners. Chessie has come a long way from his South Philly days.

Besides that I know little about Chessie's private life. Because we're both Italian, I thought he'd extend a little old-fashioned *paisano* camaraderie. But when I angle for stories, his face slams shut like a check valve.

Franny asks, "You're away on a business trip, and carry on a flirtation with a handsome co-worker. Do you tell your significant other?"

Chessie looks glumly into his beer. "I don't carry on flirtations."

"You don't go on business trips," I say.

"The hell I don't. I was in Alaska." That's another thing about Chessie: he did a stint on an icebreaker in the Coast Guard. "And even there I never had to flirt. I've never had trouble nailing a woman. What girls there were up there, I banged them."

"Inuit chicks?" Franny looks up from his magazine.

"Nah, man. These were American girls. Cheerleaders."

"Oh," Franny says.

The other mourners are paying their tabs and flapping the front panels of their jackets, birds about to take flight. My tongue feels swollen to twice its size, and I pull it out of my mouth with my fingers.

"Put that thing away," Chessie says.

"It feels weird," I say. "Does it look too big?"

Franny peers into my mouth. "You'll make some guy very happy."

"Look, don't point that at me," Chessie says. He thinks I want him. In fact, Chessie lacks the imagination necessary to conjure up a world in which not every woman wants him. But it would be more accurate to say I want to be him. Or at least, I want to have his swagger, his confidence, his ability to divine the cool from the uncool by the grace of his presence. I want to unlock that strong-box, his mind.

There on the business page is a three-column picture of our cur-rent plant manager, Margo Allshouse. The photo was snapped from a low angle to make her look tall against a distillation tower, her arms folded, her mouth set with determination. She is wearing a tailored suit and a hard hat. She's our first woman plant manager, and came to us fresh off a lockout she'd engineered downriver.

Famously, during a recent grievance procedure, Chessie jumped to his feet and said, "Lady, we make gasoline. What the hell do you do?" For weeks it was a mantra around the plant. The guys at the catalytic cracker embellished the story by having Chessie grab his crotch. On the docks they were saying he had unzipped his fly and freed his penis, flexible as a chicken's neck, to waggle at Margo Allshouse. By the time the story hit the distillation units, Margo Allshouse had yawned and said, "If you had *two* dicks I could still outfuck you, Chessie."

Now most of us think Chessie's vendetta is getting a little old, and as he starts to read aloud from the business page more of the men slap money on the bar and head for the widow's house. "The brawny Delaware Valley oil worker is becoming a thing of the past." He swallows some beer. "That's a quote. Fucking Margo Allshouse."

I pull some crumpled dollars from my skirt pocket and smooth them out on the countertop. "She assumes we don't read the busi-ness pages," I say.

"Tell me something I don't know," Chessie says.

"Okay," I say. I handle my tongue again, considering his chal-lenge. "I'll try to think of something you don't know."

I could tell him that I've seen Margo Allshouse around town, at Miss Kitty's and at Patsy's, cozying up to the bar with the other corporate dykes, wearing silk blouses and drinking ice-clear marti-nis. These are the women who laugh too loud and look around to make sure we're watching. I've always resented them encroaching on my territory, and wished they would crawl back to the B-schools they crawled out of.

Still, I once tapped on our lesbians-in-arms connection to my advantage, on a particular evening shift when I got my period and I didn't have a single tampon in my locker. A few years earlier some of us had petitioned for a Tampax dispenser in the women's change room, but as soon as we got it we busted the lock and stole all the goods, and they never restocked it. A janitor had told me that the executive women's room had tampons for free, baskets full of them, wrapped in pink wrappers and rose-scented like bouquets. They were there for the taking.

This was around the holidays and I'd been eating a lot of fatty foods, butter cookies, and bundt cakes. My flow was as thick and clotted as the grease from a Christmas duck. So I put on my coat and walked down River Drive, between the noisy cat crackers and the hissing steam lines and the jungles of dense pipe, careful to skirt the icy puddles, until the road opened to a cluster of low brick buildings: the executive offices. It was easy to break in; after big office parties we used to help ourselves to the leftover cake and punch once all the managers and secretaries were gone. Because I was the skinniest, the men usually hoisted me to a second-floor window that had been left open a crack; I could slither in and run downstairs to admit the others. On this night I was alone, but I was able to scale up the drainpipe and work my way into a conference room.

The women's bathroom was everything I dreamed it would be. A fantasy of feminine hygiene. I struggled out of my coat and dropped my coveralls to insert a tampon, suited myself up again, and stuffed every pocket with extras. I put tampons in the hip pockets and back pockets of my coveralls, in the thigh pockets where I usually carry a pair of Channellocks, in the deep, wide pockets of my Carhartt jacket. I tucked some in the sweatband of my hard hat.

The hallway smelled of disinfectant and the exit lights shone on the waxed floor. In my work clothes I felt like a dirty blight. Tampon paper rustled with every step I took. Behind me I heard a door opening, and the crustacean click of a woman's heels. I froze. The clicks came closer and I turned slowly. Because I was so stuffed with tampons, my arms were bowed like a gunslinger's. And there was Margo Allshouse.

Of course, she didn't know me from Adam. She might not have recognized that I was a woman. She saw the Carhartt, the steel-toes, the coveralls. She saw the hard hat. She saw I didn't belong there. And I suddenly remembered a story about a guy who was fired for driving out of the refinery gate with a carton of toilet paper he'd lifted from the supply shed. The men shook their heads in wonder. "Guy gave up a fifty-thousand-dollar-a-year job for thirty bucks' worth of toilet paper."

This would be my legacy. Fired for stealing tampons.

So when I saw Margo Allshouse I panicked. I figured the only chance I had was to appeal to a sense of solidarity; if I was lucky enough, she had one.

"We know each other," I said.

"Excuse me?" Her beady eyes stared a hole into me.

"You know. Like, Miss Kitty's."

I waited for a flicker of recognition, but this encounter was too far out of context for her to digest. I could see Margo Allshouse was flipping through her mental files, probably figuring out how to fire me. And I remembered the last time I had seen her someone put that old song on the jukebox, "How Lovely to Be a Woman," and she and her friends were singing along, guffawing. So I started singing it, making up the words I didn't know.

"'How lovely to be a woman'—remember?" I rolled my hips a little. "'And have one job to do, to pick out a boy and train him, and tell him what to do.'" As I sang, I backed toward the stairwell. At least I had the presence of mind not to sing a Janis Ian song, which, even facing joblessness, was more of a cliché than I could stand. Before Margo Allshouse could collect her thoughts, I was out of the building.

I told the men that story, about how I climbed in and stole tampons. I told them about seeing Margo Allshouse and my escape. But I didn't go into Miss Kitty or the song. Too much back-information can kill the anecdote.

≫

We step from the dark of the bar into the morning. It is one of those foggy cool days of a Delaware Valley autumn. Across the street there's a Wawa that sells wrinkled old hot dogs and slushy drinks; next to that is the Iron Age shoe store, now closed, and a beauty supply shop next to that. Only hookers, gimps, and bikers live in the refinery town, where the tap water tastes like diesel and the rumble from the units rattles the frame houses. My co-workers drive ten, twenty miles to treeless subdivisions where they can escape the fumes. From the plant chimneys down the hill steam rises in parallel stripes slanting across the sky toward Wilmington. The flare burns low and blue and barely visible against the mist hanging over the river. The gasoline tanks sit like fat white buttons on gray gabardine.

Franny lays a hand on my shoulder and leans heavily against me. "I have a rock in my shoe." He slips off his Florsheim and tips it; a clear tiny pebble falls to the ground. "Well, it *felt* like a rock."

I drive. Franny and Chessie climb in the backseat of my Saturn and fall asleep—Franny wheezing slightly, Chessie wagging his head back and forth as I round corners. I take River Road, past the locked-out plant Margo Allshouse left behind. The parking lot is empty except for a lone security guard. A cooling tower faces the street and the cedar louvers, once alive and springy with algae, are splintered and bleached like bones in the desert.

Larry Michalik lived on a wide flat macadam street with wide flat homes. Pickups and SUVs are parked in the driveway and along the curb outside his house. By the time we arrive the wake is in full swing.

Larry's widow sits in a folding chair drinking a tumbler of bourbon and holding a cigarette. She has short red hair and wide-set eyes. She looks like a woodpecker. Most of the co-workers gather by the server where the drinks are kept, in front of a mirror with a braided gold frame.

Chessie and Franny vanish into the crowd while I pay my respects. "I'm sorry about Larry," I say.

The widow eyes me.

"I worked on his shift," I add. Her mouth twists up at one corner in kind of a grimace. She waits for me to say something kind.

"He loved Ann-Margret," I say.

"That's the best you can do?" she says. She has a whiskey voice, like a lot of these wives.

Shouting erupts from a knot of men standing near the liquor. Franny tells the story of how he tried to fax his dick, back when we still faxed things. We'd read about a couple of women in Seattle who xeroxed their asses and faxed them around, and Franny got inspired. Standing on tiptoe, he laid his penis on the glass top of the copier and gently, gently lowered the rubber lid. Problem was, Franny had chosen the older xerox machine, with the mechanism that glided back and forth as it exposed the image, and Franny had to dance a dainty side step to keep up.

I take my leave of the widow and get a Coke to drink. Some of the wives who know me tousle my hair and tell me not to take any shit. While we are drinking, a ripple runs through the room like a breeze scuttling litter. I look over some of the men's shoulders and see that Margo Allshouse herself has arrived, an unusual thing for a manager to do. Often they'll send flowers to the funeral home, but a personal appearance is rare. Chessie turns his back to her, and as he does he happens to face me, blocking my view. "Ain't this some shit," he says, not to me in particular.

Margo Allshouse wears what she probably calls casual wear, a maroon silk blouse and wool skirt and low heels. She looks great. At once I feel ashamed of my denim skirt. Margo, of course, knows exactly the right thing for a wake—attractive, but not too sexy— and it occurs to me that if I were taller, smarter, had paid more attention in school, I might have been a power lesbian too. My bare legs glow like milk.

Everyone quiets down as Margo takes the widow's hand in hers and shakes it firmly, like a man. "Mrs. Michalik, we're so sorry about Larry. He went like a soldier."

Larry's widow examines Margo Allshouse with eyes spaced so far apart she has to turn her face one way and the other. Then she says, "One crack about Ann-Margret and I'll knock you from here to Christmas."

There's no way Margo can understand the reference—it's not as if she had any idea who Larry Michalik was or what he looked like—but she turns her wrist in a gesture of complicity and says, "I couldn't agree more. I hated *Grumpy Old Men*."

The widow says, "You and me both, sweetheart. Have some cake."

Margo Allshouse is magnificent.

Some of the wives bring her cake and the men flirt with her a little. Chessie looks over his shoulder and then smirks in my direction. When he grows angry his eyes get narrower and narrower. I've seen it happen in the plant. One time he nearly socked a pipe fitter for spreading out his tools before Chessie signed a work permit. He's prickly like that.

"Let's give her some shit," he says, over my head.

I get the feeling Chessie thinks he can handle Margo Allshouse because he lives with a divorced real estate agent, a class act. He knows women. But he's got it all wrong. Margo Allshouse is in a different league.

"Hey Margo," he calls to her. "Have a drink. Here's one more pension you won't have to worry about stealing."

Margo turns to look at him. She's walking into an ambush, and I have a sisterly instinct to warn her. But Margo cocks her head and smiles and says, "Oh, hello, Chess. I would have a drink, but apparently you've gotten a head start."

Chessie elbows aside some of the wake-goers to approach her. "Damn straight. I've been drinking all morning. I've been drinking since I read the morning paper. Seen it yet?"

Franny steps between them and spreads his pudgy fingers. "Come on, Chess. It's a wake. We're all here to have a good time."

"The Delaware Valley oil worker is becoming a thing of the past," Chessie quotes.

Margo laughs. "That isn't exactly a secret, Chess. Our future is in development and research. The oil worker is disappearing from the valley."

Chessie lifts his glass, as though he were toasting her. "You know what? That's where you're wrong. The jobs may be gone. We're still here."

"Okay," Franny says, clapping his hands together. "Let's sing a song for Larry. We could sing an Ann-Margret song. How about

'Viva Las Vegas'?" Franny moves his hips Elvis-style, twirling an imaginary hula hoop around his middle. "Huh-huh-huh," he sings. "How does it go? 'I wish there were more than twenty-four hours each day.'"

"That's the second verse, dickhead," someone says.

Chessie turns his back to Margo, his shoulders hunched forward. He emits anger, like a dog with its ears flat on its head. And Margo, Margo hunches her shoulders forward too. Even though they're ten feet apart on the living room floor, with a half dozen people singing "Viva Las Vegas" between them, they're dancing, her body responding sympathetically to his.

Then it's clear to me. Somewhere, sometime, they did fuck.

Chessie and Margo Allshouse. How did it happen? How did they make initial contact, that glancing exchange of word or gesture that establishes what each of them wants. Was it angry? Was it tender? Did he brush his hand against hers as they both reached for a doughnut in the negotiating room? Did their eruption over dental benefits and retirement plans refuse to subside until they had driven, in separate cars, to the No Tell on Route 9? Or did they plan their tryst in crisp, contractual language? And when they got there, did they take off their clothes in silence or was there groping and grunting? And those clothes! Margo's businesswoman suit, impossible to penetrate: zippers and hooks and eyelets and a double strand of pearls, support-top hose that snap like a rubber band. Once Chessie navigated all that, did she look naked and vulnerable, or, with her makeup and hairdo, did she maintain her polished enamel glaze? There's a whole grown-up world out there I know nothing about, where people have sex for reasons other than desire, like power and vengeance. I have a lot to learn.

Chessie marches out of the living room and out the front door. I think he means to slam it, but it eases shut against its hydraulic piston. No one marches out after him. The men are busy singing "How Lovely to Be a Woman" and Franny has a napkin tucked into his belt like a skirt and his hands cupped over his nipples. Margo Allshouse stares at me from across the room. Finally she recognizes me.

"How lovely to have a figure that's round instead of flat. Whenever you hear boys whistle, you're what they're whistling at."

Everyone whistles, and some of the wives stick dollar bills down Franny's pants. One of the men shouts, "You make a pretty good faggot, Fran," and, as always, my stomach convulses, a little more violently because Margo is looking at me, her eyebrow raised.

I know that look. It's the look, sympathetic and reproachful, that my friends give me when they ask, "Still not out to your co-workers, Gina?" And as I stammer that it hasn't come up, really, or that I haven't found the right time, the perfect opening, the look gets more impatient. I'm not kidding anyone. But it's easy for them; they all work in offices or schools, places where a certain decorum is expected. They don't have to listen to the sick jokes. They don't have to stand in the snow all night steaming down propane lines to keep them from freezing, hoping to get spelled for a lunch break. They don't climb tank cars or handle explosives. They don't have so much fun on the job, and they don't have as much to lose.

Margo has made her appearance. It's time for her to leave. This is her first misstep, as far as I can tell: overstaying. But she makes her way toward me, still with that cocked eyebrow, until she is standing next to me and murmurs in my ear, "You're looking at a dying breed."

I jerk my head back to look at her. With all the gaiety in the room it's hard to hear, but I'm pretty sure I got her right. I put my mouth by her ear, close enough to smell her perfume and feel her hair on my forehead, and say, "What is?"

"These men. Oil workers."

I step back and laugh. Anyone watching would think we were sharing a good joke. "*I'm* an oil worker."

Margo looks into the plastic cup she's holding and taps a fingernail against it. So she thinks we're in the same club, she and I; that's my fault. But some of the men are watching, and I don't want to stand next to her anymore. Everyone is treating Margo with courtesy, because that's the way they are, but no one's forgotten that she's the enemy.

Through the Michaliks' picture window I can see Chessie lurching about from parked car to parked car. He stands behind a BMW, apparently studying the front grille, but then I realize he's pissing.

"Is that your car?" I ask Margo.

She follows my gaze. "Son of a bitch," she says.

She puts her cup, half-empty, on the server with the other litter and goes out the door. No one stops singing to say good-bye. I watch through the window as she confronts Chessie. They both hang their heads as they speak, their necks like stalks bearing heavy fruit. Chessie removes a hand from his back pocket to point a finger at her. Then she does something that surprises me—she laughs—and climbs into her BMW. As she pulls away, Chessie manages a halfhearted wave.

The men start singing "Bye Bye Birdie," and as I head outside, Franny throws his arms around me. "Dance with me, Gina." Then he takes my hand and spins me around. Franny dances pretty well for a fat guy. When he's done spinning he presents me to the crowd, and they clap and laugh, and someone says, "Careful, Franny, she's old enough to drive."

Chessie sits on the grass, his legs straight out in front on him. As I approach him he says, "What do you do when you're not at work?"

"Me?" Chessie never lobs questions my way. I look around to see if someone's behind me.

"No, not you. Madonna."

"I don't know. Hang out." I fall on the lawn and sit beside him.

"I think you got something you're not telling us."

I jerk my head toward the spot where the Beamer was parked. "What did Margo Allshouse say to you?"

"Is that your fucking business?"

"As much as what I do in my off time is yours."

Chessie laughs. "Two points." He pulls a blade of grass from the Michaliks' lawn and sticks it between his teeth. "I know exactly what that woman needs."

So I'm wrong. They haven't fucked, and for some reason I'm a little disappointed. "Perhaps you're right," I say.

"Trust me."

Poor Chessie. All his illusions about the world are coming to an end.

It's close to noon. The street is flat and shadowless, not a living thing in sight. Only the sound of the men singing "Bye Bye Birdie," their voices rising drunkenly on "Birdie," interrupts the stillness. In a few years, after they close down the refinery and bring in the big cranes and dismantle the units and sell them for scrap, our spot along the river will be as silent and odorless as this one.

"My old man worked in the shipyard," he says.

"Mine too."

"Back then every week someone got killed. The refinery was considered the *good* job. And it was, once. Before the strike. We could do anything we wanted. Brought hookers into the plant, chilled cans of beer in the propane chiller. As long as the product was flowing, they looked the other way. Our baseball team was the best in the valley, and if a shift interfered with a game, they let us play the game. Fuck the shift."

Some of the men spill out of the house and onto the street. One of them opens the trunk of his Chrysler New Yorker and others group around. He hands out counterfeit Hummel figurines.

"You should have been there," Chessie says.

The men examine the statuettes and heft them, testing their weight. Some of them get out their wallets and hand bills to the Chrysler man. Franny starts tossing a figurine in the air, and the others follow his lead.

"Margo Allshouse is a dyke," I tell Chessie.

He snatches the blade of grass from his mouth. "Get out of here."

"Seriously."

"Well, that explains a lot." His eyes narrow. "How the hell do you know?"

"I just know."

Now all the men are throwing figurines in the air, each trying to hit the other's. I hear the Chrysler man say, "You break it, you pay for it."

Forgotten, Larry Michalik's widow staggers out of her house with a cardboard cylinder in her hand. She steps out of her mules and, barefoot, crosses the lawn in front of us toward the hedge dividing her yard from her neighbor's. "Jesus. Weeds," she says. She keeps walking and disappears between two boxwoods. The shrubbery quakes as her hoarse deep voice emerges: "Give me a hand, will you?" Chessie and I look at each other and laugh. We climb to our feet, and, curious, go to dispatch the dead.

THE SEVERAC SOUND

Water sprang from the fat penis of a bronze cherub and splashed in a turquoise pool glittering with pennies. Rachel Goldstein, no longer a kid but still looking like one, wearing a pair of flip-flops and a wraparound skirt with an Indian print, poked her hand in the stream and let it run over her fingers like cool marbles. This hotel, with its tacky fountain and parrot-colored walls, had been selected by her colleague Peter Deutsche, who murmured something about it being "so Miami." And as Rachel let the water beat against her knuckles and gazed at the statue, its potbelly reminded her of Peter himself, and she got the unpleasant sensation that *he* was urinating on her hand, so she snatched it back and dried it on her skirt.

She had spent long chunks of her life waiting for Peter Deutsche: in hotel lobbies, at airports, and on stage, where she was always early and prepared—her sheets of music open on the stand, her reeds soaking in a shot glass full of water at her feet— and where he always rushed in, huffing, at the last possible minute. Rachel was thirty-eight, Peter forty-five, but because she had known him since she was fourteen and he twenty-one, he was fixed in her mind as an older man. For seventeen of those twenty-four years she had played second oboe to Peter Deutsche's first, and had had to listen to his flourishy solos and his sexist comments about women in the audience and his bickering with the principal bassoonist. She'd watched him take humble bows (standing up straight, chin dropped to his chest, eyes closed, instrument held close to his body) when the conductor asked him to rise, and for all those years

Rachel had been left to play the second half of the concert alone, barely audible above the strings in some boring Chopin concerto while he, exhausted, rested backstage.

They were in Miami for the most sober of errands. Peter's teacher and hers, Louis (with a silent *s*) Lavigne, had leukemia, and Madame Lavigne herself had summoned the two of them, his "enfants terribles," she had said on the phone, weeping, to come say their good-byes. M. Lavigne was leaving behind legions of students. Nearly every principal chair in the country had been through the Lavigne mill at one time or another, studying at the feet of the man who had studied at the feet of the legendary Pierre Severac. But Rachel felt her visit and Peter's had particular significance, not only because they had succeeded Monsieur in his positions in the Philharmonic (he played second chair from '58 to '69, and principal after Severac's death until his retirement in '88), but because she and Peter were, she hoped, his favorites. And when Madame had telephoned her, Rachel had the distinct impression that Lavigne was waiting for them to arrive so that he could die in peace.

She chose a table outside, overlooking the pool, and as soon as she sat down a glass of juice the color of baby aspirin appeared. She shaded her eyes as if she were looking for someone. The water in the pool was ice-blue, and the ocean, beyond it, a darker blue. Blinding sunlight pounded off it. Two Jewish girls with hard tans stretched out on a couple of nearby chaises. Rachel grew up in New Jersey with girls exactly like them, tall and bosomy—girls who, when the *Diary* was assigned in the ninth grade, looked at her with heavy-lidded eyes and said, "Oh my God, you look just like Anne Frank." And if you think adolescence is tough, try enduring it as the emblem of all human suffering. At thirty-eight she looked pretty much the same: still bone-thin; still with the mess of hair, dark as granadilla, brushed back from her forehead; still with the face, a pale oval disk.

Her left pinkie started to twitch. To a stranger it might have looked like a tic, but she was actually practicing trills on an imaginary oboe, a practice that reassured her that, okay, she could still play oboe, she was still alive on this planet. Already that morning she had exercised for thirty minutes and worked on a reed in her hotel room; if she were back from Monsieur Lavigne's by two-thirty she would have time to practice for two hours, have dinner, and make another reed to fill her quota. Peter Deutsche, on the other hand, was probably just getting out of bed.

She heard his voice and turned toward the hotel. He was talking to the waiter, and when he saw her he nodded at her. He was wearing a Hawaiian shirt and cargo shorts, and his thinning blond hair was damp with comb marks. When Peter was a young man he moved like a much older man—fat boys will do that—and now that he was middle aged he moved like someone from another era. Courtly. Peter wasn't so fat, really, just loose and lardish, like unrisen dough. He made his way through the tables and pulled out the chair next to hers, scraping the patio.

"Look what I got," he said. He placed on the table a Ziploc bag of uncut cane, the raw material for their reeds, which they ordered from France by the pound.

"Cane?" Rachel asked.

"*Cuban* cane." He looked from side to side. "Contraband. This morning I went to see this guy in Hialeah whose grandmother ships it every month. Top dollar, but it's worth it." He unsealed the bag and held it under her nose. "Smell."

Rachel sniffed. The green smell of fresh cane knotted her stomach.

"Great, huh? This is primo stuff. But I shouldn't be flaunting it." He clamped down on the seal with his rolly fingers and slipped the cane on his lap. "Señor, dos cafés, por favor."

"We're in America, you know," Rachel said.

"Barely. Besides, they like it when you speak their language."

She slumped back in her chair. "So did you try making a reed with that stuff?"

"Here?" He blew air from his lips dismissively. "I didn't even bring my oboe."

"God, Peter. We're here for three days."

"It's too humid. Any reed you make here will be worthless back in New York."

Rachel thought of the hour she had spent shaping a reed that morning and scratched her nose.

"You didn't," Peter said. "Christ, Rachel, what were you thinking? This weather is hell on your instrument. My advice is to put your oboe in a plastic bag with a piece of orange peel. It'll soak up all the excess moisture."

Peter knew, among other things, that William Herschel, who had discovered Uranus, was also an accomplished oboist. He knew that Hawaii had risen from the sea as a chain of volcanoes, the difference between laser and dot matrix, and the names of all the Supreme Court justices. How he learned all this was a mystery, since Rachel had never once observed him express the tiniest bit of curiosity about anyone or anything.

The waiter brought their coffee and Peter ordered bacon and eggs. Rachel wasn't hungry. She watched Peter rigorously polish his fork with his napkin and hold it up to the sunlight.

"So," he said, "I'm thinking you should go see Lavigne first." He looked at her and said, "Were you thinking we should go together?"

"I didn't make any plans."

"He might be confused. It's better this way."

She wanted to ask, why do I go first? It was so Peter could make a grand entrance—her visit was a warm-up to the big event. But when Peter made an assertion, there was no space to argue. He sort of used up all the oxygen.

"Give them some time to rest between visits," he continued. "I figure you get out of there at one, and I'll show up at two. And I've made dinner reservations for us tonight at this place in South Bay I read about."

"I have to practice tonight," Rachel said.

"Give it up, Goldstein."

There was a time, in her early twenties, when she had had sexual fantasies about Peter Deutsche. Rough, punishing stuff: German and Jew locked in mutual loathing. The fantasies ebbed as she got to know him better. And anyway, Peter's taste ran to Koreans, string players, with golden apple cheeks and raspberry stains like huge hickeys on their necks where they held their instruments.

She watched him shove eggs in his mouth as he continued talking. "This Cuban who sold me the cane kept house with an old guy, a piano player. I guess they had some homo thing going on. And the old guy had some stories. He once played with Billy Strayhorn."

Rachel's left hand twitched: an F-sharp scale. Peter glared at her and laid his knife and fork across his plate.

"Don't tell me you don't know who Billy Strayhorn is."

She shrugged.

"Duke Ellington's arranger. They *called* him an arranger. Some people say he actually wrote most of Ellington's songs, but he never got credit. He was gay and stayed in the background."

"Okay Duke Ellington I've heard of."

"I'm so proud of you." He picked up his utensils and continued eating.

When they finished breakfast, Peter asked the concierge to call a cab for Rachel. The driver had a rosary and a soft-focus cardboard picture of Elian Gonzalez hanging from his rear-view mirror. She was angry—angry that Peter Deutsche had scooted her off first, but angry most of all that he hadn't brought his oboe with him. Three days without practicing. But Peter always got away with murder. She still burned to think of the night, seven years earlier, when Simon Rattle was guest-conducting *Le tombeau de Couperin*, with its big oboe solo. As he was unpacking his instrument Peter turned to her and said, "I forgot my good reed. Can you spare one?"

Who forgets a reed? Who *borrows* a reed? She wanted to protest that if he were stupid enough to leave his reeds at home, he should forfeit his solo and let her shine for a change. But she silently opened her cigarette case of reeds, all so lovingly created they had faces and personalities, like children. She picked one that had given her some trouble in the higher registers— a stubborn, mischievous boy. Let Peter Deutsche tame it. She handed it to him and he stuck it between his lips and blew a cracked, cawing noise. "This will do," he said. *Do*, as if it were Rachel's function to furnish him with reeds. And when at the end of the piece Rattle pointed his baton at Peter Deutsche and the audience roared as he stood and did his chin-dropped-eyes-closed routine, Rachel found herself constitutionally incapable of looking at him. Instead she raised her eyes to the acoustic tiles suspended in the rafters above them, saw the wires snap and a tile crashing down and crushing Peter Deutsche's soft round skull.

On its way to the Lavignes' retirement community, the cab crossed a bridge over a marshy inlet and they entered a development of condos. No sidewalk, no stores, just townhouses rising from the bog like fen grasses. As if out of respect for the elderly, the driver turned down the salsa music on the radio. Under the best of circumstances, a trip to see Lavigne made Rachel's nerves flutter. This was worse. He was sick, and sickness had never been her strong suit.

He was just Lou Levine, Sergeant Lou Levine of Brooklyn, when he was discharged from the Army. Sergeant Levine fought in Normandy, and when the war was over he decided to stay in France, study his instrument, and rent a room over a butcher's shop in Pigalle. Paris appealed to him: the vulgarity, the stone walls from which sprung tiny rivulets and beds of moss, the loud cafés at night where Monsieur, who wore his dignity like a silk handkerchief, cut a quiet figure, kind and approachable. Lots of GIs stayed in Paris, but Lou Levine was ardent enough to make his name look more French and marry the butcher's daughter. And he sought out Pierre Severac, who was already on the far side of middle age and suffering the malaise of war.

What was the oboe before Pierre Severac? A duck's quack, a squeak, a sound so choked and ugly it made the rest of the orchestra sound full by its very smallness. A child's whine. Back in those days musicians didn't work on reeds. They bound two pieces of cane together, blew on them, and threw them out: that was the German way. But Severac attended to his reeds with cobblerlike craftsmanship, shaped them full at the base, translucent as nacre at the tip. And what came out was not a quack at all, but a song.

It was M. Lavigne who rehabilitated him. Europe, he argued, was too exhausted to appreciate Severac. He brought him back to New York, where Bernstein was creating a new American sound, strong and virile, and Severac became its backbone. Lavigne played beside him, second chair to his teacher's first, succeeding him after his death. But perhaps Lavigne's greatest legacy was as the apostle of the Severac sound, the full-throated sexy tone that came to characterize the American orchestra.

Rachel had memorized all of this history even before she auditioned for him. She sat beside her mother as they entered the Lincoln Tunnel from New Jersey, her instrument heavy on her lap. "Look, just play like you always do," her mother was saying, taking her right hand off the wheel to wave it in the air. "Of course once he hears you, he'll be dying to teach you. You've been all-state two years in a row. But go easy on the vibrato, and don't take the Britten too fast. And please don't slouch." She ran her hand down Rachel's spine and pinched a lower vertebra. Rachel studied the ceramic tiles on the arched roof of the tunnel and thought about the tons of pressure from the Hudson River swirling above their heads. What would it take for the tunnel to buckle beneath the weight? For the river itself to rush in and toss the cars like jetsam? Drowning didn't scare her. Emerging into the sunlight of Manhattan did.

That was the first day she entered the Lavignes' West End Avenue apartment, dark, crammed with figurines and objets d'art and smelling like boiled cabbage. Rachel stood at a music stand in the living room, on a spot of Oriental rug worn thin by M. Lavigne's previous students. As she arranged her selections on the stand her mother perched on the edge of the overstuffed sofa. "She started with clarinet and we knew she had to keep going. She showed such talent. So she's been studying with the teacher in Fort Lee. I mean, he's very nice, but—" Her mother held up a hand in dismay. "It just wouldn't be fair to Rachel, not to go further. She plays as well as he does."

M. Lavigne listened with his head slightly cocked, a king indulging a subject. How old must he have been then? Fifty-seven, fifty-eight? Young by orchestra standards. Yet she regarded him as an old man. Rachel studied the pattern in the rug, a design she would still see, twenty-four years later, whenever she closed her eyes. M. Lavigne pressed his fingers together in a steeple shape and said, "You must forgive me."

"Excuse me?" Her mother was caught up short.

"I get a bit nervous during auditions, and make it a house rule that no one sit in other than the auditioner and myself. That way, if I say something utterly fatuous, there are fewer people to hear it."

"You want me to leave?"

"There's an excellent coffee shop downstairs. Their black-and-white cookies are simply not to be missed." When her mother was out the door, he nodded to Rachel and said, "Well then, Miss Goldstein, what have you prepared?" And gratitude washed over her like a blush.

Her relationship with M. Lavigne was mostly played out in her imagination. Their lessons were professional and awkward; the only affection thrown her way was from Madame, who served tea and cookies afterward. But he was a looming presence: a raised eyebrow, an impatient cough could spin her into despair one week, and a quiet "That was fine" the next would be parsed for days. Did fine mean good, or adequate, or elegant? Too fancy, too thin? When Rachel selected her lunch at the school cafeteria she heard his voice: milk, excellent, excellent choice; an apple, most refreshing.

For three years she stood on the threadbare spot on the carpet and played for him. At the beginning of her senior year, M. Lavigne asked her what her plans were, and she recited the speech she had gone over so many times in her mind: she was applying to liberal arts colleges with strong music programs, like Indiana and Oberlin, with the goal of continuing her music while acquiring a skill in a related field—music therapy, maybe, or education. When she finished her cheeks burned. It was the longest paragraph she had ever spoken for him.

Monsieur made his familiar steeple shape with his hands, and rested its peak on the bridge of the nose. He disapproved.

"Yes, you *could* do that, I suppose," he said finally. "Or you could come to Juilliard and study with me."

Rachel's heart stopped. She was seventeen and old enough to know that, outside of novels, people's lives did not reverse in a moment. But he continued talking, arranging her funding, describing the paperwork, explaining the curriculum. Later, in Madame's kitchen, she could barely sit still for tea and cookies. When she left the apartment she had to walk all the way back to Penn Station just to burn off energy. She cut through Lincoln Center, lingering in front of each of the framed posters announcing the winter concerts. She was now part of this rarefied world. She sat on the black granite fountain and ran her fingers through the water. It was late autumn. The only other people at the fountain were a pair of Puerto Rican teenagers—a girl, shyly ducking her head, and a boy in a Mets cap with his arm around her—and a stout Indian woman with a toddler, her purple sari resplendent with mirrors like the eyes of peacock feathers, who let the toddler run around and around the fountain. When Rachel was nine she spent a golden afternoon at the community swimming pool with a boy she adored, and he made her laugh so hard she forgot there was a world outside the aquamarine rectangle and the sunshine and the two of them. Because of that experience she was able to recognize the emotion: she was drenched. From this point on life would be excellent; she was no longer the girl from New Jersey but the latest in a long line of legends—Lavigne, Severac, Bernstein himself—and her teacher was grooming her, perhaps to sit beside him as second chair, as he had sat beside his teacher. Perhaps ultimately to succeed him. She was being brought into the fold.

Of course she hadn't calculated on the pudgy blond boy from the Pennsylvania Dutch country, who was just finishing up at Juilliard as she was starting, making such a stink with his graduation recital. When Lavigne retired to Florida, eight years later, it was Peter who ascended, and Rachel ended up a permanent second chair, aging every year in a job that was supposed to have been transitional. And as the cab driver weaved through the sunny streets of the development, she realized she was going to see him not to say good-bye but to dispel once and for all the misery that had dogged her for so many years. She needed to hear him say that *she* was his prize student, that it was an accident of birth order that had ordained Peter as principal and her as second chair.

All the townhouses looked alike. Rachel guessed who might live in this retirement community—aged salesmen and accountants—and it seemed to her a sad kind of anonymity for someone of Louis Lavigne's stature to end up here. His neighbors probably had no idea who was among them. She paid the cabbie and let him drive off, and stood outside for a moment, tense, as she used to be going up in the elevator on West End Avenue. She was a grown woman, middle-aged even, but in front of her teacher she was a perpetual fourteen.

The doorbell was loud and clanging. She couldn't imagine he would like that. A fake-cut-glass diamond window was set in the door. A dog barked from a neighbor's house. For a second Rachel was seized with panic, a sense that she was missing something. Then she realized she had never, ever once approached the Lavigne home without her oboe in her hand, like a talisman.

Madame opened the door and flung her arms. "Rachel! *Cherie*. You have not changed one bit. What is your secret?" She folded Rachel in her arms.

"*You* haven't changed, Madame." It was true. Mme Lavigne had grayed a little, but other than that she was the same as always: the prim topknot, the blue eye shadow, the scent of Chanel No. 5. Madame's cheek was moist and oily against Rachel's.

"Nonsense! He has been sitting by the window all morning waiting for you."

Rachel's heart skipped like a lover's.

"All week, such visitors we have had. It has been—" She spread her arms to show the magnanimity. "But you and Peter were always special."

On closer look, Madame had aged a bit. Hairline creases radiated from her mouth, and her tea-rose lipstick bled into them.

Rachel expected the bourgeois clutter of the Lavignes' dark West End apartment to be transferred to Florida: the Oriental rug, the tattered books, the elongated African masks and porcelain statuettes and framed Degas. But the Florida home was alien, clean and spare and sunny and smelling not of cabbage but of Lysol. They stood in a foyer on a parquet floor. Rachel saw the kitchen to the right and, to the left, a carpeted hall leading to other rooms. She realized that Monsieur would not be quite himself either. He would be gray and dying and strapped to IV lines.

"Go, go!" Madame flung her fingers as if she were scattering droplets.

Rachel headed into the cool white of the hallway and saw an open door at its end. She stopped before it and craned her neck to peek in.

"Well, Miss Goldstein. How good to see you."

He wasn't bad. He was sitting up, on the edge of his bed, in a pair of crisply ironed cream-colored pajamas. His slippers dangled from his feet. There was only one IV stand in the room with a full bag of clear liquid hanging from it, but Monsieur was not plugged in.

"Hey." She sidestepped into the room and automatically reached to unpack the oboe case she had not brought. "How are you feeling?"

He tilted his head. "Not so bad."

"You look fine."

She sat on a cane-bottomed chair facing the bed. The visitor's chair. Through the window she could see the identical houses on the treeless street and beyond them, the blue of the inlet. "This is a nice place," she said. "I've never visited you here before."

"A van comes to take you shopping, or to cultural events in Miami. It's very convenient."

Rachel nodded and let her gaze take in the room. On the dresser sat the portable 78 player, the only sign of their former bohemian life. "I remember that record player." She stepped toward it and stroked its base. A stack of dense black discs was on the spindle.

"I made Pauline dig it out of the closet so I could listen to some old recordings." He lifted a finger, long and elegant. "These are some rare records Severac made when he was in Paris under the Vichy."

Rachel snorted. "He played for the Vichy?"

"Ours is not to judge, Rachel."

"I know." Chastened, she removed her hand from the phonograph player as if it were on fire.

"Go ahead and put one on."

The portable had rectangular brown buttons and panels lined with a coarse canvas. The arm was heavy, and she placed it carefully in the groove. It was Rossini. The sound was a little scratchy, with all those ambient noises the old 78s picked up: a chair scraping against the floor, the squeak of fingers against strings, a wind player gasping for air. In a moment Severac emerged in a solo, one he later made famous in his Philharmonic days. But what came out of the 78 was nothing like the music he made with Bernstein. His sound was thin and hoarse, slightly flat. It was a kazoo. Why would

Severac make a record with such a bad reed? She looked at Lavigne for an explanation.

"Cane was hard to come by during the war," he said. "The Germans had ruined the fields in the south, and trade with South America was suspended. Oboists had to use anything, anything they could come by. Most of it was junk."

Rachel accepted this and sat down. She was surprised that Monsieur felt he had to continue.

"Even after the war, provisions were scarce. Severac and I found a vintner outside Lyon we could work with. He used cane to protect his grapes and, for a price, spared some for us. It wasn't the best, but it was better than what was coming out of Germany. I spent hours working with it. Pauline's father sharpened my knives till they were like a barber's razor. I realized that if I got the reed down to a fingernail's width at the tip and kept it full in the back, I could get a good, full crow. I showed him"—he bowed his head toward the portable—"and he agreed it was an improvement."

He was quiet for a moment, and Rachel realized he was giving her time to absorb information.

Then he took in a quick breath and said, "You have to understand the conditions he was working under. And the Germans! Glorified oompah bands. All brass. What kind of poison influence that must have been."

She stared. His skin was so white it was translucent. She could see tiny blue veins in his eyelids.

"*You* invented the Severac sound," she said.

"Well, he was responsible for bringing it to the world. I was no one then, just an ex-GI who had never attended conservatory or played in a major orchestra. If he hadn't been so generous—"

"He ripped you off." Her throat tightened and her pinkie twitched. "All those years, taking credit for what you did."

"Actually, he helped my career immeasurably."

He pressed his fingertips together. The record ended, and the arm clicked and returned to its cradle. Rachel's heart pounded with rage. Severac! Lavigne was relegated to playing beside him, year after year, forced to watch Severac shake spit from his oboe, play solo after solo, take credit for Lavigne's own innovation. How did he contain himself? Even after Severac's death, how could he resist the impulse to scream about it in the middle of Lincoln Center?

The music was followed by silence: no sirens, no dogs barking, no noises from the kitchen. He had once told her that, when Verdi was dying, the people of Milan lined the streets of his neighborhood with straw to muffle the clomp of horses' hooves. Lavigne deserved such a tribute.

"If it's quite all right, I think I'll take a nap," he said. "Peter Deutsche is visiting this afternoon. I love the boy, of course. But he can be rather exhausting."

Rachel nodded. At the mention of Peter's name she remembered what she had come for: the affirmation that she was his favorite, no matter what their seating order was. But she knew that "exhausting" would be the most damning indictment M. Lavigne would offer. That was okay; in light of Lavigne's troubles, her own seemed dwarfed. She was ashamed.

"I need you to help me lie down," he said. It was a directive, like playing an A-flat scale or toning down her vibrato. He made no apologies. "The best way is to lift my feet and swing them on the bed," he said evenly.

She nodded and knelt. His heels were shiny and calloused, crisscrossed by tiny white lines, but the skin on his calves was as brittle as papyrus. "Do you want your slippers on or off?"

"Keep them on," he said, and she was relieved. The sight of his naked toes was more than she could endure. She snapped the elastic around the back of each foot and lightly wrapped her hands around his ankles. They were as small as wrists. She understood, then, that he was dying, and even though she had seen him only sporadically the last few years his presence in the world made it a softer place, more inhabitable.

"Okay," she said. "Ready?"

"Go ahead." She lifted his legs, shocked by their buoyancy, while he braced himself, leaning back on his elbows, and watched her hands. She lowered his feet on the bed, careful to center them. Then she moved to his head and put her hand between his shoulder blades. Instinctively he resisted her, so she held him up with one hand while with the other she lifted his left arm, then his right, crossed them on his chest, and gently laid him down. He closed his eyes and said, "Thank you for coming, Miss Goldstein," just as he used to when their lessons were over. Her signal to leave.

Peter Deutsche ordered white wine and warned her that eating seviche at this time of year she'd run the risk of contracting hepatitis; stuffed trout was the better choice. They sat on a patio in South Beach, in front of a deco-looking building. A citronella candle in a red cup covered with netting burned between them. Cars blasting hip-hop stopped at the traffic light near them; when they drove off she could hear the ocean.

"Shall we get cocktails?" he said.

"With wine? I fear not." I fear not. Why did she talk like that when she was around him? Her voice was glass grinding glass.

Peter smirked. "Live a little." He put his finger in the air. "Muchacho, dos margaritas, por favor."

"Oh my God. So much for practicing tonight."

"One night. Think you'll survive?"

"I guess." But her stomach burned.

Their drinks were pale green and foamy. Peter had changed into a new Hawaiian shirt. He lifted his glass. "To Louis Lavigne."

She hoisted her glass.

"A great musician, a great teacher, and the last of the real gentlemen," he said.

Rachel waited for the punch line, but Peter's face was dead serious, even passionate. He held his drink aloft and waited for her toast.

"Here, here," she said. They touched glasses and sipped their drinks. Hers was sweet and sour, and she immediately felt lightheaded. "Wow."

"Good, isn't it?"

She nodded and placed the glass on her cocktail napkin. "I don't drink very much." She turned toward the street and pretended to be deep in thought. She heard Peter take another sip.

"So," he said, "did he play that shitty Severac record for you?"

She continued staring. She had expected to feel jealous, but she was grateful Peter knew about Severac. It was too enormous a revelation to bear by herself. She looked at him and said, "What do we *do* with that?"

"Do?"

"I mean, shouldn't we tell someone?"

"Who should we tell?"

"I don't know." Her voice was pleading. "A music critic. That historian who wrote the book about the orchestra. Lavigne should get credit."

Peter thought about this, turning a matchbook over and over in his fingers. "We could tell our students," he said. "Beyond that, who cares, really? Some band geeks and orchestra queens. Just because the modern reed is everything to us doesn't mean it has any importance out there." He pointed the matchbook toward the street, where a long white limo was pulling away from the curb.

"He shaped the sound of the American orchestra."

"Well, not single-handedly."

She slumped in her chair and swallowed more of her margarita.

"Who wouldn't want to go out this way?" Peter asked. "Attended by the woman who's loved him for sixty years, students flying in from every corner of the country to pay tribute. The mark of the good life."

"I guess."

After dinner they walked along the beach. There was moonlight, and Peter carried his Converse sneakers in his hand, and if Rachel hadn't kept an awkward foot of space between them, a passerby might have thought they were enjoying a romantic stroll.

"I was lucky I found lilacs this morning at the hotel florist," Peter said. "Pauline's crazy about them."

"You bought her flowers?"

"Of course."

Rachel plowed her toes into the sand. "You might have told me."

"Why? Was I supposed to get you flowers too?"

"I mean, I didn't bring anything."

"That's not my fault," Peter said.

They walked a little farther. Her flip-flops kicked granules onto the backs of her shins. "That's true," she said. "I never know how to act."

Peter didn't say anything, and she imagined him shrugging beside her. He broke into a trot and charged up a dune, toward the water.

"Where are you going?" she asked. She followed up the dune and, at its crest, saw Peter at the water's edge removing his clothes. He hopped on one foot as he pulled the other through his shorts. He was very white, with a hard, round belly that he carried as if he were proud of it, like a pregnancy. He held his shirt by the collar and let it flap in the breeze. Beyond him phosphorescent breakers emerged and vanished in the dark.

"Let's go for a swim," he called to her.

Rachel stumbled down the slope, trying not to look at his penis. "Now?"

Peter laid his clothes on the sand and laughed. He ran into the waves and disappeared, then resurfaced shooting a long stream of water from his mouth. "It's great," he called. "I love the ocean."

Peter loved the ocean. Peter loved Cohibas and single-malt Scotch. Peter loved the Motherwells at the Met and Mahler's Ninth—the world was just a big china bowl full of things that Peter loved. It was easy for Rachel to be cynical: after all, what did she love? Not playing the oboe. Not Mozart, not anymore. Not the sound of the trumpeters as they warmed up in the last moments before the houselights dimmed.

She loved Louis Lavigne.

While Peter Deutsche frolicked in front of her she saw her future as flat as the horizon. Within a week they would be on stage together, and Peter would be leaning back in his chair, perilously close to tipping over (but never close enough), telling the bassoon section the story of their trip to Florida, how Peter brought lilacs for Madame, how Lavigne played for *him* the Severac record, how Peter then celebrated Lavigne's life with a skinny dip in the ocean but how she, Rachel, was too inhibited. She trembled with anger just anticipating it, knowing how badly she would want to cover his mouth with her hands, kick the chair out from under him, make him shut up. So she acted preemptively and took off her clothes.

Disrobing was easy enough: she untied her wrap skirt and let it drop to the ground, crossed her arms and peeled off her top, slid her panties past her ankles, and stepped out of her flip-flops. She felt a slight salt breeze on body parts that had never before been exposed to fresh air: it rustled her pubic hairs; her backside felt cool. It was new. She stepped toward the ocean and let the water run up around her ankles as the sand, grainy and scratchy, sucked her feet. A shell hit her instep.

Peter Deutsche swam underwater, a dark shadow like a shark, and popped up, flopped on his back, and paddled with fussy flip-perlike hand motions. Rachel advanced slowly. The water reached the middle of her calf, then her knee, then her thighs.

"Why, Miss Goldstein. What perky little breasts you have."

She cut a karate chop in the water, splashing him. Peter laughed and sank below the surface. He emerged four feet away. "The crotch line is the toughest part," he said. "It's easier just to jump in."

She hugged herself and grinned. Her splashing left beads of water on her arms. Even if she ventured no further, she had foiled his expectations. And what right did he have to expectations, anyway? Consider all the secrets she knew about him: that he came to concerts hungover or exhausted from a night of sex, unpracticed, that he sight-read through rehearsals. Not that any of it mattered. Because she had to admit, even on the night he played *Le tombeau de Couperin* with her bad-boy reed, the night she went home and pounded fist-sized bruises into her thighs, rapturous with rage—even on that night, he played so well she wept: better than Severac, better than Lavigne. Peter had a sinuous sound that wrapped around a melody and slid under its skin: knowing, sensual, smirking. And she knew, serviceable as she was, she would never play like that, no matter how hard she worked, no matter how much of an asshole he was. Peter was quite simply an oboist like she'd never be. This was not a transitory condition, like the alignment of planets. This was fixed for all time. And somehow she had always known that the moment she admitted this would be the moment the earth opened up and swallowed her; the futility of her life would steamroller her and leave her flattened. But instead the ocean lifted her by the armpits and pitched her forward. She tumbled headlong into the surf, a disposable piece of human flotsam. A greenish blackness enveloped her, and the lights from the shore flipped over and disappeared, her hair fanning like seaweed; the sound of her own burbling filled her ears, loud as an ovation. She somersaulted backwards once, then twice, scraping the sea bottom with her belly. She did not struggle. Her limbs went dead. In the next second the wave receded, and she found herself standing waist-deep in the water, salt stinging her eyes and throat and sinuses.

Peter swam around her in a circle. "Isn't it great?" he said.

She spit and rubbed her eyes, nodding.

"I told you. Now try floating on your back."

And she let herself fall back, caught by the sea; she lifted her feet until she found an equilibrium. The water rocked her. Her muscles relaxed. From the air she and Peter must have looked like twin rafts, bobbing in sync—one with a big white belly, the other with hipbones like crescendo marks pointing toward the sky. The Miami lights blotted out most of the stars, but she saw Venus, and the moon, and felt the tide nudge her toward safety as it lapped around the Florida coast, as surely as it receded from the coast of Europe.

MUSCLE MEMORY

If Destiny had three wishes to make, the third would be that she could learn to weld. The first two, which involved her father coming back to life and things returning to the way they used to be, would never come true, but learning to weld was a possibility. She just had to get off her ass and decide to do it.

Her father had been a welder, up to a couple of years ago when he died. Drowned. But once upon a time he used to come home from work earlier than the other daddies, the bill of his cap still turned backward, his skin smelling of hot metal and acetylene, his forearms covered with white scars like splattered paint. At night he would sit in the kitchen with his buddies from the shipyard and play dominoes, slapping tiles on the table and talking trash. As she did her homework in the rear room she could hear their voices bubbling with music. Her mother, who was a nurse at Charity, didn't have the energy or the spirit to invite her friends to the house. It was all she could do to come home and soothe her feet in a salt bath.

Destiny was eighteen. She and her mother lived in a house without neighbors. Occasionally a masterless dog would trot down the street, clicking its paws on the pavement, and turn his curious face to their house as he passed. Their view—once crowded with houses, churches, bars, and a corner store where the little kids bought Slim Jims after school—now let them see straight to where the levee used to be, and in the daytime they could watch ice chests and laundry baskets bobbing in the canal like buoys.

Destiny worked in a tool crib at the same shipyard that once employed her father, across the river in Jefferson Parish. She spent the day in a cage, signing out boxes of hex nuts and fittings of galvanized steel. Whenever a new boy would start work on the ship, a tacker or a pipe fitter's helper, he would come to the crib asking for a skyhook or a left-handed screwdriver or an automatic crescent wrench. It was her job to break him in, to tell the rookie that his co-workers were just messing with him, that there was no such thing as a skyhook, and after she eased his embarrassment, she watched from her cage as the boy went back up the elevator and onto the ship. The tool crib was, for most of the day, a lonely place, and the pay was the lowest in the yard. She had to learn a skill.

"What you want to do is you want to talk to Augustine Beaudry. That's what you want to do," said Shelton Binns. He was a pipe fitter, about thirty, with a face as smooth as a Frenchman's. When he leaned across her counter she could smell his cologne. "He's taught about half the welders up there."

"For real?"

"I got no reason to lie. See what you gotta do is on your lunch break go on up to the ship and ask him to teach you. You're not going to learn anything stuck down here."

Even though she had been working in the yard for four months, she had never gone up to the ship. It was ten blocks long, docked in its berth, elephant-colored, its skins glaring with sunlight and filling her field of vision. Upriver floated two more crafts just like it. The shipbuilding business was good.

The ship frightened her a little, only because it was so large, and because she watched so many men (and some women too) disappear into its depths every day: one second, at shift change, the yard was full of people, chatting and laughing—country people, Cajuns who came up from Houma, and old-timers who were staying with family all the way in Picayune or Biloxi; and, more recently, Mexicans, with their dusty ball caps and their *mira-mira* talk, who lived in makeshift trailer parks over in Plaquemines Parish and who climbed into the crane cabs or steered the forklifts up and down the docks. (Shelton Binns said he wasn't prejudiced, but he wondered if it was such a good idea for the Mexicans to be running the cranes and the forklifts, as they had different safety standards down there; it was a whole different system.) Then the next second all this jabber was silent, and only Destiny and a couple of expediters were left on dry land. The sudden depopulation spooked her. It was as if they had all died until quitting time. But she knew Shelton was right, and she had to go up to the ship. No fairy godmother was about to show up in the tool crib and teach her to weld.

The elevator was a little red cage with a plywood floor, operated by a one-armed coonass named Guilfoyle. His gums were black and his teeth were yellow against his blotched white skin. He clanged the door shut behind her and pulled on the lever with his one arm and they started up with a jolt, running so close to the hot surface of the ship she could have poked her finger through the mesh and touched it.

Guilfoyle had a stack of egg cartons at his feet.

"Hard-boiled egg?" he snarled.

Destiny shook her head.

"Twenty-five cents. Five for one dollar."

"No thank you."

He kicked a hatbox next to the eggs. "Praline?" He said it the coonass way. *Pwa-ween.* He was really country. "Fifty cents each. No exceptions!"

"No thank you."

As they reached the main deck Destiny felt as if they were peeking over the walls of a hidden city. Workers darted around. Hoses streamed across the deck, grinders planed their wheels this way and that, throwing off cascades of orange sparks. Propane bottles in canvas slings dangled from overhead hoists. The hot white glow of the welders (Destiny knew to shield her eyes) burned off to the side. Men shouted warnings to each other: Watch your back! Boom on the right! Women, tackers, looking tough with their caps turned back and their kerchiefs knotted around their necks, dropped the stubs of welding rods from their clamps onto the floor and ground out the embers with their steel-toed boots.

"Here we is," Guilfoyle said. He slid open the door and Destiny stepped out. All around her: noise, heat, and the cheerful sound of people at work. Destiny looked for a familiar face, like Shelton's, but finding none, opted for a group of men who had spread their bandannas on the floor of the deck for an improvised picnic.

"Hey," she said.

The men looked up, not scary. They were peeling hard-boiled eggs and wiping the little triangles of shell and skin on their kerchiefs. "Hey."

"You know where I can find Augustine Beaudry?"

One of the men made a face. "Now that's a shame. What's a beautiful young girl like you looking for a beat-up old piece of shit like that for?"

"I need to ask him to teach me to weld."

"I see." The man speaking rubbed his chin. "What you want to do is climb down to the ballast tank."

"The what?"

"Come over here." He stood up and turned her fore. "See that hole in the deck? Climb down that ladder. That's what you call the ballast tank. You'll find Augustine Beaudry right down there."

She thanked him and as she walked away she knew their eyes were on her. Her old boyfriend used to say, Baby, when you walk it's like your hips are the Atlantic and the Pacific fighting it out between them. She was tall, and even in her work clothes she looked good. The tackers cut their eyes at her as she passed.

"Good luck," one of the men shouted.

She descended to the ballast tank on an iron ladder. The tank was cramped, but at least ten workers were down there, grinding and burning. An enormous exhaust fan sat at the end sucking fumes into a large duct. Everything sounded louder here, and she had to watch her footing, taking care not to get tangled in the ropes and hoses.

"You know where I can find Augustine Beaudry?"

"That's him right there."

Augustine was a hard-looking man, with a permanent frown and nasty shave bumps and a mustache with gray in it. His welding mask was pushed back on his head, and he held a fresh rod in his clamp. "Well?" he said.

"You Augustine Beaudry? They told me you could teach me to weld."

"That's what they told you?"

"Yes."

"You want to be a tacker?"

"No sir. I want to be a full-fledged welder."

"Oh, I see. A *full-fledged* welder." A couple of men standing by him, small and hunched, started to cackle. "And what do I get out of this?"

"Excuse me?"

"I understand what you get. But what do I get? You want to take my time, my expertise, probably my welding gear, too. But here you come without so much as an egg, and you could have gotten that in the elevator."

"You want an egg?"

More cackling. Augustine rubbed his forehead with his knuckle. "Come back when you're serious."

That evening, as she helped with her mother's footbath, Destiny asked her who taught her father how to weld.

"I don't think anyone taught him. He picked it up. He was gifted in that regard."

Destiny knew her father was gifted, but she was always suspicious when people told her they just "picked up" a skill, like French or playing the guitar, almost as though they were ashamed of the hard work that went into it.

"Well, where did he pick it up? Was he at the shipyard already?"

"Oh, no. It was something he learned as a boy. Over at his cousin's, if I'm not mistaken. Baby, what's wrong? You want to learn to weld?"

"Some of those welders make twenty-five dollars an hour," Destiny said. "I'm only making nine." She squeezed a washcloth so the water ran down her mother's damaged legs. "You could start thinking about retiring."

"Well, I don't want you to do it on my account. I remember your father waking up in the middle of the night feeling like someone threw sand in his eyes."

Destiny knew all about that, but it seemed like a small price to pay. While her mother dried off, Destiny sat down to read a magazine, and as she landed on the sofa, she heard the crackle of paper. She reached between the pillows and pulled out a Snickers bar. Her mother always discouraged candy in the house. She wondered how long ago it had been lost, and from whose pocket.

When Destiny returned to the ballast tank, she opened her hand to reveal a large brown egg. Augustine took it from her without thanks and turned away.

"Hey," she said. "You wanted an egg. Now you got it."

"Like I said, back when you're serious."

The third day she bought a praline from the coonass, who with his one arm fished it out of the hatbox at his feet. It was in a baggie sealed with an electrician's tie-wrap.

"Here." She presented the praline to Augustine.

He grunted and took it from her.

"You gonna teach me now?"

He tore open the bag and popped the praline in his mouth. "You're gonna have to try harder than this, girl."

She had a mind to ask him to spit out the praline into her hand, if he wasn't going to keep his end of the bargain. But she turned and climbed out of the ballast tank.

"I'm not surprised he's acting ornery," Shelton said, when she told him her troubles. "You know who he is, don't you?"

"You mean besides being Augustine Beaudry?"

"I mean he is *the* Augustine Beaudry. From the Scorchers."

"The what?"

"Oh, man. You're so young you don't even remember. You ever hear a song called 'Hell and High Water'?"

"Sure. My father used to listen to that."

"Now see, he had good taste. Well, Augustine Beaudry, that's the man who used to sing it."

"What?" She turned toward the glare of the ship and blinked. "What's he doing in there? They play that song on the oldies radio all the time."

"Well, you know. They didn't pay royalties back then. A group would go into the studio and get five, six thousand dollars for cutting a record. That was considered good money."

"Man." She could see why he was a little cranky. All that money being made off his song, and he wasn't seeing a dime.

On the way home she stopped at an old record shop on Magazine Street. "Do you have anything by the Scorchers?" The boy she asked had a sunken chest and a scraggly beard. He struck a pose, one hand on his waist and the other on his chin. Then he put his finger in the air and said, "Hell and High Water!"

"Yeah, that's it."

"If we do," he said, leading her down one of the long aisles, "it'd be over here." He flipped through some old LPs in a bin. "Here it is."

The cover featured five men in tuxedoes against a lilac background. She studied their faces. The second from the left might have been Augustine, although his face was rounder. But the one all the way on the right—that was him. He was smiling, so he was hard to recognize. And he was thirty years younger, of course. "How much?"

The boy removed the disc from its cover and balanced it on his fingertips, checking for warps and scratches. "Three dollars."

At home, Destiny set up her father's old hi-fi to listen to the record. "Ma, do you remember the Scorchers?"

"'Hell and High Water.' Of course I do. Time was your daddy and I used to hear them play over at the Maple Leaf. 'Hell and High Water' was what put them on the map, but I always preferred another song they did, called 'I'll Take Fire.'" Splashing her feet, she sang. "Some men drown from lonesomeness, some men burn up with desire. Baby I know how I will die between fire and water, I'll take fire."

"That's a spooky song."

"Reminds me of those old blues they used to do."

Destiny looked for the track on the record and lowered the needle into the groove. The song had a kind of hollow sound to it, as though it had been recorded at the bottom of a tin can. She tried to connect the high, yearning tenor voice coming out of the speakers with the grumpy old man in the hole. When the song was over she went to pee, and when she flushed she heard a clatter in the tank. She lifted the lid and found two cans of stewed tomatoes bobbing alongside the float.

≽

The next day she put the record album in a plastic Safeway bag and hung it from her wrist as she lowered herself into the ballast tank.

"What do you have for me?" Augustine said.

She pulled the record from the bag and handed him a pen. "I was hoping to get your autograph."

He took the record from her and turned it over, looked at the back cover, then turned it back to the front. "Where in hell did you get this?"

"Magazine Street." She didn't tell him it cost her three dollars.

"You like 'Hell and High Water,' I suppose."

" 'S all right. But what I really like is 'I'll Take Fire.' "

He stared at her hard. "So you like a good ballad, then?"

"I guess."

He took the pen from her and scribbled his name. "I told them that should have been the A-side. They wanted to go with something more upbeat." He gave her the pen and the record. "You're the girl they call Density."

"Destiny," she corrected.

"So you're looking to be a welder?"

"Yes sir."

"It's a very, very honorable occupation," he said. "You take something that isn't there and turn it into steel."

"I know."

"You got a welding hood or do you expect me to supply that too?"

"No, I got a hood. My daddy's."

"Won't your daddy be needing it?"

"He's gone."

"I see. Bring your hood and gloves tomorrow and we'll see what we can do."

The hood was right where her father had left it, hooked on a nail in the garage, just inches over the watermark. Mildew grew over the walls like ivy. She buried her face in its plastic hollow and smelled the ash. There weren't any scorch marks on the inside of the hood—it was curved like an eggshell, made to hold her face. She looked for any stubborn remains: whiskers, dandruff, streaks of salt from his sweat, anything that attested to his having been alive. But the hood was clean. She might have known; he did not often leave a mess behind.

It was two weeks before they found Destiny's father, washed up beneath a bridge by St. Claude Avenue. At least they believed it was him. His body was bloated and purple, his shirt buttons popped and his clothes in shreds, his skin filleted and peeling in thick wrinkled layers like a soggy roll of toilet paper. An inspector laid him out in the animal shelter they were using as a morgue and suggested they check dental records for a positive identification, but their dentist had run off to somewhere in Arkansas and left his records behind in a filing cabinet that had by now floated into the sea.

The corpse's fingers were so swollen they had engulfed his wedding ring the way a tree will grow around a chain-link fence. The inspector offered to cut his finger off.

"That's all right," her mother had said. "I know who it is."

For a long time Destiny thought her mother might be wrong. After all, the corpse did not smell like her father. It smelled like wet garbage, rotting apple cores, spoiled corn, and vomit. Her father had the hot, dry smell of burning metal, an aroma she so closely identified with him she figured he was born with it. It took her weeks to comprehend that a man's smell will die with him. Now she knew.

Destiny ratcheted the headband of her father's welding hood tight around her head. With a sharp nod she dropped the mask and she saw nothing. She lifted it and the moldy garage was still around her. Sharp nod: nothing. Lifted the mask, everything was the same. Looking for his gloves, she opened the drawer of his old Kennedy tool chest and found rows of Peppermint Patties, shining like silver dollars. They fit perfectly in the drawer, three deep and five across, as if they were in a display case. She removed one of them, upsetting the pattern, unwrapped it, and popped the candy in her mouth. The peppermint oil burned her tongue.

At her first lesson, Augustine set up two pieces of scrap metal in a vise so that the seam between them was narrow and long. He straightened the lead, whipping it like a cowboy's lasso, and pulled a fresh rod from his quiver. Inspecting the clamp, Destiny saw there were different grooves she could fit the rod into, so it would be angled up, angled down, straight ahead, or at a perfect ninety. She tried different positions and settled on angling the rod up.

"Finished playing?" Augustine said.

"I'm all right."

"All right then. Pretend like you're going to strike an arc but don't make contact."

She pawed at the air with her welding rod.

"What you want to do is stroke the surface of the metal lightly. Stay in one spot too long and that rod'll freeze up on you. Too fast and you won't get a spark. But once you nod down that hood you won't be able to see a thing. You'll be alone in the darkness. So get a sense now of where that metal is and how far you got to reach it. Clear?"

"Yes."

"All right then, let's go." They dropped their masks by nodding sharply. Everything around her went black. She could hear voices and the buzz of a grinder, but they seemed distant, on the other side of an ocean. The smell of her father's hood reassured her. She poked the welding rod toward the metal, and a shock zapped her arm. The rod was jammed.

"Froze it! Lift your mask," Augustine said.

She lifted her mask and released her clamp. The rod was sticking to the metal like an arrow in flesh.

One of the little hunched men said, "Whoo, whoo! Indian attack!"

Augustine twisted the rod loose. He threw it on the ground. "I told you, you gotta keep that tip moving." He produced a fresh rod.

Destiny tried the different grooves. Pointing up, pointing down, pointing straight ahead. "What way do I put it in?"

"That's what I asked *her* last night," one of the little men jeered.

Augustine scowled. "It don't matter a goddamn which way you put it in there. Just quit messing around and get to work."

She slid the rod in a groove, pantomimed striking the arc a couple of times, and snapped her mask shut. She reached into the darkness. Zap. Her arm buzzed. Froze again. This went on for a good fifteen minutes as Destiny ruined one perfectly good rod after another. Then Augustine said, "That's enough for today."

"I didn't even strike an arc yet."

"It's your first day. What the hell did you expect?" He sat on a twelve-inch duct and motioned for her to sit by him. Then he pulled an egg from his breast pocket and peeled it.

"So what kind of music you listen to, mostly? Hip-hop?" he asked.

"Mostly I guess."

"Any old school?"

"Well, you know. What my parents liked. Earth, Wind and Fire."

Augustine stared hard into the distance. "What about the music from around here?"

"You mean like the Nevilles? All right."

"You young people shouldn't forget. You're the only ones who can remember."

"All right."

"Do you know who Screamin' Jay Hawkins is?"

She shook her head. Augustine pulled apart the white of the egg and sucked the yolk out of its socket.

"I want you to find out." As he talked he showed his yellow-coated tongue and Destiny had to look away. "You come back to-morrow and we'll continue your lesson."

It meant going out of her way to Xavier and using the library computer. She found a website about Screamin' Jay Hawkins and scrolled through it quickly. It was weird and ancient stuff.

That night she shook off the moldiness by listening to her favorite DJ, Yolanda, send out her late-night love dedications on Q93. Yolanda used to end every show by saying, "To all my boys offshore tonight, Yolanda sends you a big wet kiss. Mmmwwaah." Nowadays she said, "To all of you on land and at sea, wherever you are, Yolanda misses you and sends you a big wet kiss." It made Destiny both happy and sad to think of all the people who were listening at the same time.

The next day she said, "That was one strange brother."

"Who is that?" Augustine asked.

"Screamin' Jay Hawkins. Big hit: 'I Put a Spell on You.' Which he used to perform from an *actual* coffin."

"He did, too." Augustine chuckled. "I caught him with a lady in a quilted Eterna-Rest 5000 more than once."

"Oh, no, he did not."

Augustine's eyes were shining, and she could see he was pleased. As she tried to strike an arc, he spoke to her gently through the darkness. "Don't try too hard," he said. "If you try too hard you defeat your own purpose. Just stroke it like you're tickling a baby's belly."

Destiny zapped a couple of more times and sighed deeply as Augustine twisted the fresh rods off the metal. But he was not impatient. The third time a small red light glowed, and it illuminated the seam, the rod, even the vise, and a fragile, concave, silver pool of flux spread beneath her hand. Then the surface of the pool trembled and cracked, and the light snuffed out.

"I *had* it," she said, lifting her visor. "I had it for a second."

Augustine bent down to inspect the seam. "You did, too. Look at that there."

A slender silver bridge slung like a canopy between the two edges of metal. It was sloppy. But it was welding. Destiny put her hand to her hood, but Augustine said, "That's enough for today. Tomorrow I want you to tell me about Fats Domino."

An hour later, when Shelton came by the tool crib to chat, the phone on the wall rang. "Supplies and expedition," she said.

"Density."

"Destiny," she corrected.

"Who's that you're talking to?" Augustine's voice was thick and gruff on the line.

Destiny squinted and looked out the window. "How you know I'm talking to somebody?"

"You better watch yourself."

She hung up. "Fool."

"Augustine Beaudry?" Shelton asked.

"How does he know what I'm doing?"

Shelton shook his head. "Augustine's one pack of Camels short of a carton. It's like the water picked him up and set him down someplace else."

That afternoon her mother went to Algiers to talk to people from the government. Destiny took a look around her room while she was gone. Everything was in order: the framed pictures on the vanity of Destiny and her father and grandparents, her mother's hairbrush, a Bible, a *Physicians' Desk Reference*. The floorboards turned up at the corners and squeaked when she stepped on them.

She was sneaking around on her own mother. She didn't like doing it, but she snuck anyway. She opened the closet. On the right side, her mother's scrubs, pink sets and green sets and one printed with Shrek characters, for the occasional pediatric rotation. On the left side, dresses for church and luncheons. Destiny put her hands between the dress section and the scrub section and parted them. Behind the clothing she found tins stacked from floor to ceiling. Hawaiian pineapple, cocktail franks, barley soup, mandarin oranges, corned beef hash, smoked oysters. Also jars of Zatarain's mustard and clam juice. No two foods that would actually make a meal together.

Destiny went out for a walk. She wanted to hurt somebody. On Prieur Street she saw a dead frog splayed on the sidewalk. She kicked it like a football. At the home of the Landrys, whose daughter was two years older than Destiny, a fish skeleton was washed against the front door. The block smelled of rotting cabbage and wet plaster. Then she smelled something like burning rubber and went toward it, across Caffin Avenue, past an abandoned FEMA trailer with its door slung open and, inside, a tricycle with plastic streamers hanging from its handlebars, past a house twisted off its axis, past a single Air Jordan on the curb, a few busted pallets, and a dog carcass that shimmered with maggots. When she saw where the smell was coming from, she was surprised to find a live person, a man of about fifty in a purple velour tracksuit, arms crossed, watching a greasy oil drum fire. She stood beside him and helped him watch.

"What are you burning?" she asked after a while.

"All of it."

Once Destiny learned to strike an arc, she guessed it was only a question of weeks until she would be a welder. She had run long distance in high school, and she knew what it meant to persevere, to practice every day until she mastered the task. But welding had a different learning curve. Every day she went up in the elevator and down into the ballast tank, and every day she buried herself in the dark and worked on whatever old chunks of metal Augustine had scrounged up for her, and then one of two things would happen: the red glow of her arc would sputter and extinguish, and she would raise her hood to find a trickle of flux like birdshit sucked into the seam, or the glow would deepen and rage out of control, and instead of joining two pieces of metal she would drive them farther apart, their jagged edges gaping like the red gates of hell. She was willing to try again, but instead of scavenging new scrap metal Augustine preferred to sit her down and deliver his sermon for the day on Ernie K-Doe or Professor Longhair. She had no time to improve.

If she had a good day Augustine would share the egg she had bought for him, cracking it open and handing her half the egg white.

"What do you think it means," Destiny asked, trying to sound casual, "if people hide food all around the house?"

Augustine chewed his yolk, bunching up his lips as he chewed. "You hiding food?"

"Not me. I'm talking hypotheticals."

"Hypotheticals," he repeated. He swallowed his yolk so she could hear it. "Usually it means somebody's been acquainted with hunger. Hypothetically speaking."

Destiny watched the little men lower buckets of water into the ballast tank.

"There's a lot of people around here," Augustine said, "doing things they didn't used to do."

Every day she looked up the old-timers he assigned. She understood what he was trying to do, to connect her to her roots and give her a sense of belonging to something big. But listening to that musty music did not make her feel connected. It made her feel alone. Destiny wanted to hear what other people were hearing. Living people.

"How's your welding coming?" her mother asked as Destiny sponged her legs.

Destiny shrugged. "I thought after this many weeks I'd get the hang of it. Be better at it, anyway. It's like I'm not improving."

"Oh, it just seems that way."

Destiny felt desperation rising in her throat. She wanted to ask, what will happen to us if I can't learn a real skill?

Her mother ran her fingers over Destiny's scalp in a way that made her feel five years old and coddled.

"It just seems like you're not improving, but you are," her mother said. "It was the same way when I had to learn how to take blood. I used to stick and stick and stick. Lord, I bruised those patients black and blue with all my clumsiness. Then, lo and behold, one day I just did it. Simplest thing in the world, like I'd been doing it all my life. It just takes time to burn a new habit into your muscle memory, is all."

Destiny knew her mother was trying to be encouraging, but she also knew that welding would never be the simplest thing in the world. As she trickled water over her mother's knees, a boom rattled the windows. They looked at each other.

"Sounds like the Hayes house," her mother said. The house across the street.

Destiny's mother stepped out of the footbath and hurried to the front room. Her arches were so high and regal she left wet prints like question marks on the floor. Destiny followed.

The Hayes house had collapsed. The walls and windows were gone. The gutter of the roof rested on the ground, and through the rising smoke Destiny could see white four-foot letters painted on the shingles. "Two Alive."

One day Augustine asked her, "You go to dances, proms and such?"

"Proms? I graduated from high school last year." She tried not to sound exasperated. She still needed him to teach her to weld.

"You go to clubs? Where do you go to hear music?"

"Clubs sometimes. Parties." Destiny drew a fresh rod from a box to show him she was concentrating on her work. "Most of my friends aren't here anymore."

"I bet you could get me a gig."

"A gig?"

"Someplace where young people are."

Destiny dropped her mask. Instead of arguing she struck an arc and focused on welding.

When Shelton came to visit her that afternoon he turned her wrist and inspected the soft underside of her forearm. "You're getting scars. Looking like a welder."

Destiny withdrew her arm to her side of the cage.

"Don't hide it, girl. You're supposed to be proud of your battle scars."

He thought she was hiding because she was ashamed of her scars. She was hiding because she still wasn't a welder. The scars lied.

The phone rang and she said, "What?"

"Who sang 'Wish Someone Would Care'?" Augustine asked.

"Irma Thomas."

"What was the B-side?"

Destiny sighed. "I don't know what the B-side was. Now go do your job and let me do mine."

When she hung up, Shelton said, "He always knows when I'm here."

"I better get back to work," she said. "I got a shipment of copper tubing to log in."

Augustine had a habit of asking Destiny a question just as she was about to drop her visor. He was like a boy needing attention. And he was getting worse with his pestering. Destiny was getting the idea he didn't want her to learn how to weld so much as keep him company.

"You remember to get me a gig?" he demanded.

"I never promised you that. You think I know people. I don't know anyone."

"Hell you don't. You're a pretty young girl. Pretty young girls know people."

"I don't." She used to. Now she had so few people in her life she was about to die of suffocation. She dropped her mask, and Augustine knocked on it. "What is it?" She lifted the visor. "I gotta practice."

"I spend my valuable time here setting up your lessons every day I expect something in return."

What valuable time? She looked at the metal scraps in the vise— two round discs that a burner had cut from a pipe and left on the floor. Big deal.

"I already told you, I don't know anyone. I can't make something out of nothing."

"I bet you haven't even tried. People remember 'Hell and High Water.' "

"Then go ask one of them." Her face grew hot.

"They don't owe me like you do." One of the little men cackled, so happy Destiny thought he was about to dance a jig.

"I don't owe you nothing, old man. And you know what else? There ain't nobody wants to listen to what you have to offer."

As soon as she said it she was sorry. She remembered the young hipster in the record store putting his finger in the air and saying, "Hell and High Water!" Lots of people remembered. But Destiny was so annoyed she didn't want to admit it. Something drove her forward. "Your music is older than whaleshit, and anyone who ever liked it is dead."

Augustine's pupils constricted. "That's what you think."

She turned from him, lowered her visor, and struck her arc. There it was, the low red glow, the silver pond like a sunken belly. She teased it out by making a figure eight with the tip of her rod and there, a second, interlinking pond, exactly the same size. Then another, and another, descending rings of silver. It was easy. She sealed off the bead with a final flourish, like a period to her sentence, and pulled away. When she lifted her mask Augustine and the little men were back at work, ignoring her. She drew her little triangular hammer from her belt and chipped away at the slag. Underneath was a perfect bead, not too fat and not too skinny. She spat on it and watched the saliva skitter across the hot surface, then picked up a stiff wire brush and shined the bead until the silver reflected reds and blues. It was beautiful. And it was hers. She knew in her arms that she could do it again. Anytime and anywhere.

Augustine saw her admiring her work. He came over to look at her bead.

"Feeling pretty good, are you?"

"Pretty good."

"Think you're some kind of welder?"

"It's looking that way."

"Hell." He stepped across the tank and picked a torch up off the floor. With his thumb he opened the gas valve, and then he lit the jet with a Bic lighter so a steady blue flame like a laser flowed from its mouth. Then, squinting, he aimed the torch at her beautiful silver bead. She watched it melt and disappear into the seam of the discs.

"There," he said, turning down the flame. "Try again."

The two of them looked at where her weld had been. She wasn't angry. But she knew to hang around him anymore was to sink fast. "You know what?" Destiny said. Her heart pounded. "I can't help you."

"*You* can't help *me?*" Augustine said, mimicking her. The little men around him started to laugh, and as she climbed up the ladder she could hear their voices echoing in the ballast tank. On the main deck she felt a salty wind blowing up from the Gulf. A gang of riggers scurried beneath an overhead crane swinging a sharp sheet of metal from fore to aft. She didn't mind the tackers giving her dirty looks. They were just tackers. She was a welder.

Three weeks later she took her examination. An inspector with an X-ray machine scanned her weld like a baby in its mother's belly, and, satisfied with its density, proclaimed her a welder. "Pretty soon your handiwork will be going off to Eye-Rack or Eye-Ran," he said.

When she got home she taped her welding certificate to the refrigerator. Then she cleaned out her mother's closet, stacking up cans of food and packages of ramen noodles on the front step. She was still stacking them up when her mother came home from work. "We can bring these to the homeless shelter," she said.

"Oh, well," her mother said. She said it as if she were running late for church. *Oh, well.*

"I passed my welding test." Destiny sounded angry.

"I knew you would."

"I can *buy* you anything you want. Anything you're hungry for."

"That's just a little something in case of an emergency." Her mother picked up a box of spaghetti and rattled it, close to her ear. "It doesn't hurt to keep this around, does it?"

Destiny bent over and straightened a pile of boxes. "It takes up room."

Her mother sighed. "I just keep thinking. If we had been a little more prepared last time we could have saved ourselves a whole ocean of trouble."

Destiny picked up a bag of elbow macaroni that had fallen out of a carton. When she was a little girl she used to listen to her father say, "Taking responsibility, Baby: that's the hardest thing to do." Now she knew that, in this one thing, at least, he was wrong. Taking responsibility was easy. Learn a trade, train your hands to do something they couldn't do before. The hard part was all the ruination that lay outside of your responsibility.

Destiny's family had brought what they thought they needed to the roof. It would be like a beach picnic—they would eat crackers and drink from a ninety-ounce bottle of orange soda and watch the water rise and fall with the tug of the moon. Sooner or later help would come. Only help didn't come. At night they tried to sleep on the pitched tar shingles and listened to the noises of the neighborhood shut down, one by one. A dog quit barking. A far-off car alarm went silent. And a long, angry back-and-forth between a mother and son stopped suddenly and deafeningly. As her father rolled up his pant legs on the third morning, getting ready to go look for food, he told jokes about catching fish in the floodwaters. And Destiny, her head pounding from thirst and sunstroke, rolled her eyes.

But she was not the same person now that she was on that roof—anyone could see that. Her shoulders were widening and straining against the seams of her T-shirt. When she crooked her arm her biceps were hard as billiard balls. Her throat burned and her mouth tasted of flux, and now and then her retinas lit up with a flash so white she could see the blood vessels of her own eyeballs. Not only that, she had a head crammed with voices, songs, and singers that she hadn't even known a few weeks earlier, all kinds of jerky rhythms and crazy instruments.

Destiny's mother ran her finger around and around the ridge of a can of pears. "Baby, I *know* you can provide."

"What is the issue then, exactly?" Destiny glared at her mother.

"When I wake up at night it gives me some comfort, looking at these cans." Destiny's mother turned the pears over in her hand. Then she fit her finger into the metal ring at the top of the can, bent it back, and peeled the lid off. She fished a piece of fruit out and passed it over to Destiny.

The pear was a soft molten white, heavy with juice. Destiny hesitated for a moment, holding the fruit, and then she took a bite. The sweetness spread across her tongue and for a moment she felt like crying.

From somewhere, on the next street over, maybe, or the street after that, a radio played an accordion tune. Destiny couldn't imagine where the music could be coming from; what houses still stood on the block were abandoned, their doors swollen and busted from their frames. Across the street a turtle the size of a manhole cover crawled from the wreckage of the Hayes place back into the gutter.

"All right," she told her mother, the sweetness still in the back of her throat. "Maybe then you'll let me build you something to put them on. Just so they're not all over the floor. I can weld some brackets right to the wall, so you don't even have to get out of bed."

Destiny's mother smiled. She took another piece of fruit and slid it between her own lips, then carried the can back into the house.

The song in the distance was a Boozoo Chavis two-step, Destiny knew. Rounder Records. She strained to hear more as she picked up the supplies, once more, to return them to her mother. She had the bill of her ball cap turned to the back and her bandanna around her neck, and she pushed her sleeves back on her arms, admiring her scars. Propping the screen door open with her foot, she wrapped her hands around four cans of red beans and listened for the record to end and the next one to begin. She knew all the songs and artists before the announcer named them, and she could sing all the words.

SEND ME WORK

Harriet knew the party was over two days before Christmas, 1983—the day her best friend, Israel the clown, unexpectedly blew in from Sarasota. Harriet had lost her job, her boyfriend, and her apartment in a single eight-hour span, so when Izzy appeared, as if telepathically summoned, she expected him to save what had been an exceptionally bad day. It was his occupation, after all, to restore good spirits: he worked for the circus. When they were kids, Izzy had tried to teach her to ride a unicycle in Prospect Park, his hand gripping the banana seat as she lurched forward and back. "Okay," he had said. "I'm letting go now."

"Don't let go!" Harriet had squealed.

The job she lost was just a temp gig in an accounting firm where she operated an antique Burroughs posting machine, and although she loved its gunmetal smell and the red-and-black spool of ribbon, Harriet knew that the accountants had to reconcile their losses by the end of the year and that she'd be canceled along with their other debits.

Losing the boyfriend wasn't so bad either, even if he looked a little like Pacino. He called himself a writer, but he spent most of his days lurking around the Strand checking out the first sentences of novels. The apartment, though, was a honey. A rent-controlled West Village one-bedroom overlooking a courtyard. Very *Rear Window*. When he evicted her, the boyfriend threw his keys on the kitchen table and said, "You and I inhabit completely separate simulacra." It was late afternoon. The sky hung low and pewterish, threatening snow. Harriet packed her belongings in a red patent-leather hatbox she'd found on the curb of Perry Street and smoothed her bangs on her forehead. She was going through a Louise Brooks phase.

But she realized she was at the close of an era not because she lost her job, or her boyfriend, or her flat. It was because, as she swung her hatbox on her way to a Hudson Street pay phone, taking inventory of her friends who had spare sofas or floor space, she couldn't come up with a single name. At least, no one so intimate she could show up at his door, having squandered her last money on a bottle of tequila and a bag of limes, to say, "I just got fired and dispossessed; let's celebrate." Standing on the corner of Christopher and Hudson she finally understood that all the boys had vanished, like children in a dark fairy tale. One by one, each of them had complained of a minor ailment—a scab on the knee, a tongue coated with thrush—and before Harriet knew it they had left town, retreated to the dreadful places they had once escaped. Dover, Delaware. Tupelo, Mississippi. Steamboat Springs. If she sent a birthday card it returned unopened, sometimes with a frosty note from the boy's parents scrawled on the envelope, and Harriet would study the return-to-sender stamp for some indication of whether the boy were dead or alive.

She grieved for these boys, and shuddered to think of their last, lonely days. And she felt abandoned. Standing on the corner beneath the low clouds, her hand on the sticky pay phone, was like standing at the foot of a well, with a girded, moss-slick bucket dangling over her head. Harriet looking up at it from the cold muddy bottom, calling, Hello, hello? Can anybody hear? Hello?

She telephoned her sister in Brooklyn.

"You can stay for one week," the sister said, before Harriet even asked.

Harriet heard the baby cooing in the background. Harriet liked the baby all right, and how her skull had the spongy texture of a pound cake, but she dreaded her sister's disapproval.

"I know you've been thrown out," the sister continued. "Israel already phoned here looking for you. He called your apartment and was told you don't live there anymore."

"Izzy's in town?" Harriet's mood lifted. Just when she was in free fall Izzy threw her a line. He had a spooky sense of when to call in the middle of the night or send a newsy letter.

Harriet wrote a phone number on the back of her hand and dropped another quarter in the slot. A young man answered and Harriet asked to speak to Israel. The boy dropped the phone, and she heard what sounded like furniture moving on the other end of the line. Then she heard Izzy's voice, that soft scratchy timbre that reminded her of old Victrolas.

"Well, he kicked me out, Iz." With her toe she nudged one of the used rubbers that littered Christopher Street. "*And* I lost my temp job. If we're going out you're treating. So who's the boy who answered the phone?"

"Classified info."

"You can't say. Okay, buddy. Can you get away?"

"Any time you say."

"Sheridan Square. Thirty minutes." She didn't even have to say which corner of Sheridan Square. He knew. Izzy came to New York several times a year, sometimes visiting his father, the rabbi, sometimes not, and sometimes dating some man or other he'd met on the road. But always he made time for Harriet so they could roam around the city. With thirty minutes to kill she headed toward Seventh Avenue to watch the holiday lights emerge against the darkening sky. The sidewalks were full, in spite of all the men who had gone missing, and she bobbed through the crowds like a cork. She passed a sex toy shop decorated for the season with a garland of red and green foil condom wrappers strung on a fake white tree. She got tangled in the leash of a Chihuahua tethered to a parking meter. On Washington Street, a fortyish man in a houndstooth coat sat behind a bridge table piled high with books and videotapes and milk crates crammed with record albums. Another estate sale. Christmas shoppers were flipping through the albums. She picked up a book—something about the Harlem Renaissance—and picked up an album cover. It was Harry Belafonte's *Calypso*, its edges soft and frayed. With the record in her hand she tried to absorb the energy of its past owner. "He sure had eclectic tastes," she said.

The man in the houndstooth coat waved his hand at her. "You don't know the half of it."

Izzy, she noted, would want to hear about the tables full of books and records, the sidewalk sales that were sprouting up around the neighborhood. He was lucky to be living in Florida, far from the plague.

As kids they used to spend every weekend rambling around Manhattan, or sitting like grown-ups watching Harold Lloyd one-reelers at a film lovers' club in the basement of the Plaza Hotel. A redheaded waitress brought them ginger ale in highball glasses, each with a sophisticated maraschino cherry. As the afternoon closed in and dusk started to settle they walked along these very streets of the West Village, peering into the warm lemony windows of the brownstones, picking out which house they would live in when they were older. Who knew that at thirty she would still be looking in from the outside?

She decided to go ahead to Sheridan Square and wait for him, like a girl waiting for a boy in an old wartime movie. She was even dressed for the part, wearing a nubbly brown coat she'd gotten for ten dollars at a thrift shop in Gramercy Park. It had a faint stain on the lapel but it was plenty warm and had a coffee-colored lining she adored. Underneath was a 1964-era Mary Quant (six bucks), navy with white accents and perfect for work, with a retro touch of irony that Israel would appreciate.

And there he was. Punctual as ever, Izzy had reached their meeting spot first: she could pick him out from across Seventh Avenue. No mistaking that oversized army coat and the duffel bag at his feet. Israel may have been a Jewish boy from Brooklyn, but when he visited from out of town these days he affected the look of a soldier on leave or a rodeo rider lost in the city. The traffic light changed and she surged forward with the crowd, eager to reach him. Then she stopped dead, right in the crosswalk. Maybe that wasn't Izzy after all. The profile didn't look right. His hair, thick and auburn, was cropped short as a Marine's, only uneven, with neglected patches here and there. And the face was too thin, actually gaunt. But the flattened tip of the nose was definitely Izzy, and the way he leaned against the three-mouthed fire hydrant, one foot propped up behind him, his knee bent at an improbably flexible 180°. The big army jacket looked bigger than usual. While she was frozen there the traffic light changed again and taxis honked. He turned to her and his arm shot up in the air. It was Izzy all right. He had a scab over his eyebrow the size of a Ping-Pong ball. The strength in her legs gave way, and she would have sunk to the pavement if a pedestrian hadn't jostled her.

"Well, if it isn't Harriet the spy," Izzy said.

Wobbling, she threw her arm around him and pressed her face against his neck. He was as slight as a paper doll.

"Now, now," he said, patting her on the shoulder. "Let's have a lovely evening."

"Evening?" she asked. She'd been counting on spending the next few days with him. "How long are you in town?"

"I've got an eleven-thirty flight out of LaGuardia."

"Tonight? You're only here for one day?"

"I've already been here for three. It's all the excitement I can stand."

"And didn't call me till now, you bum?"

Izzy looked up Seventh Avenue. "Let's get some dinner, hey?"

So that's how it was going to be. He didn't want to talk about it. They never did, these boys. It was some fraternity Harriet couldn't join. He hoisted his duffel from the sidewalk and slung it over his shoulder. She took his arm, careful not to squeeze. She had long comforted herself to think that Israel was imperishable, always cautious and discreet, even a little prudish.

"Okay. So if you've been in town for three days, what *have* you been doing? Never mind. I don't want to know." She tried to tamp down the tremble in her voice.

"Actually, I've been a good boy." He tapped her wrist. "*Have* to be. What have I been doing? This and that. I went to the new television museum. You can sit at a monitor and watch any program from any time, ever. I watched some old Red Skelton shows."

"By yourself?" Harriet envied his capacity for solitude.

She steered him to a Thai restaurant, warm with the smell of curry and hot peppers. It was still early, not even six, and the place was nearly empty. When the hostess looked at Izzy her face softened, and she led them to a booth by the window. Izzy shook off his army coat and sat opposite Harriet. He wore a red plaid flannel shirt and its shoulder seams dropped halfway to his elbows. His Adam's apple was pointy. Izzy had been a pretty boy, with peachy cheeks and plush lips, and now his lips were thin and dry.

He leaned across the table and fingered the collar of her Mary Quant. "Look at you. So *That Girl*."

"I thought you'd like it."

"You should be prancing down Broadway with a parasol." He shook out his napkin and laid it on his lap. "So what's going on?"

"Come on. I don't want to talk about me, Izzy." Her troubles were pretty small.

"But that's my job."

Harriet took his hand from her collar and kissed it. "Golly, Iz, you seem a long way off."

"Well, hell, then. Come and sit next to me over here." He slid toward the window. She jumped up, moved his duffel to the opposite bank, and scooted in next to him. They sat hip to hip, like lovers, the side of her foot pressed against his.

"That's better, isn't it?" he asked. She nodded, reveling in his nearness. As kids they had sleepovers until they were ten or eleven and their parents started to object. They lay under the covers together, kicking the blankets to create sparks, giggling with the coziness of their limbs side by side. As long as they could sit this way, knee to knee, elbow to elbow, she could keep from flying apart.

"Okay," he said, "gossip with me."

"I'm starving," she said. She opened her menu.

"How's your career?"

"I euthanized it. I've come to the conclusion that you're the clown in this partnership. Not me." She had liked writing the jokes, actually, but the audiences were dense and brutal, and her long, intricately detailed stories made them impatient, and her Barbara Stanwyck impressions soared clear over their heads. Mostly stand-up involved hanging out in bars with a bunch of belching hetero jerks, waiting for three minutes at the mic.

"You were funny," he said. "Not belly-laugh funny, but gentle, understated."

"People don't pay a two-drink minimum for understatement."

"That's their loss," Izzy said. "Anyway, I think you and I have a duty to cheer people up."

"*You* do," Harriet said. "You're the lucky one. You were born with that clown gene. You always knew."

"Lucky?" he asked. "Care to trade?"

Chastened, Harriet shut her mouth. For the first time in her life she did not know how to talk to him. The hostess came with two sizzling trays of curry, even though Harriet didn't remember ordering.

"That looks really good," Izzy said, half to the girl, half to Harriet. His voice was light. She knew he was reassuring her: it was safe to chat.

"Okay," she said, "so there's this disc jockey on BAI who plays a whole show of misconstrued lyrics." Harriet sharpened her chopsticks. "Listeners call in with the lyrics they've always heard wrong, and then he corrects them and plays the record. Guess what his theme song is?"

Izzy shoved some food around his plate. "'Excuse me while I kiss this guy.'"

"Good guess! But no: 'There's a bathroom on the right.'"

"Creedence Clearwater."

"Precisely. So this guy calls in with the Springsteen song, the one about driving all night just to buy you some shoes."

"Oh, I love that. So romantic." Izzy twirled his chopsticks in the air, as if he were churning up some romance.

"Isn't it? It starts out, 'I wish God would send me word, send me something I'm afraid to lose.' And this dude always heard it, 'I wish God would send me *work*, send me something I'm afraid to *do*.'"

"I like that version better."

"Me too," Harriet said. "I've been singing it that way all week."

"Very elegant. Very subtle."

Slowly the restaurant filled up. Bridge and tunnel people. Kids from Brooklyn like they used to be, firefighters with their families, Mafia ladies with spidery mascara. Also locals: gay couples on dates, law students, jewelers.

"Did you see your father this visit?" Harriet asked.

"Nope."

End of discussion. It was a sore point, Izzy and his father. Harriet wasn't even sure if Izzy had come out to his dad and she didn't ask.

The rabbi had marched in Selma. A picture of him crossing the Edmund Pettis Bridge, locking arms with Martin Luther King, hung over the leather couch in his office, and as a child Harriet used to kneel on the sofa to study the photograph while Israel rehearsed pratfalls off the desk. The rabbi had pointy eyebrows and an eagle nose and long earlobes that seemed always to sprout a day's growth of stubble (ear-shaving courtesy of *Mrs.* Rabbi Shapiro, Harriet assumed, since deceased). Harriet was always a little afraid of him.

Sitting next to her now in the light of the Thai restaurant, the rosiness gone from his lips and face and his skin dry as paper, Israel had come to resemble his father in a way she would not have predicted. And she could see the middle-aged man Izzy wouldn't become, principled like his father but milder and less disapproving.

She leaned into Izzy as he played with his food. Steam fogged the windows, and above their heads a tiny handprint emerged on the plate glass.

"Look at that," she said.

Izzy looked up. "What do you know." He reached to touch it. "So small. Must have been a baby."

"How did it get all the way up there?"

"His parent must have lifted him," Izzy said, "to look out onto the street. To watch the parade of people. Kids like that. Watching activity, bustling. That's why they like clowns."

Harriet watched the little handprint grow clearer as the mist thickened. The girl came to take their platters. Their food was mostly untouched. Harriet grabbed the lip of her plate and said, "Wait, I'm not done."

The waitress took Izzy's curry away, while another girl walked around the room lighting candles on the tables. Harriet's face grew warm. She was suddenly flush with happiness. Her future came into sharp focus and it involved Izzy and palm trees and the blue Gulf of Mexico. The answer for both of them was simple. They had to go on sitting next to each other, arms and hips touching like twins.

"You know what?" she said. "Me losing my job and my boyfriend and my *apartment* and all. Maybe it couldn't have come at a better time. In fact, maybe it's a sign."

Izzy took a tin of Drum tobacco from his jacket with some cigarette papers. "A sign?" He sprinkled tobacco leaves into a paper and rolled it, rocking the cigarette back and forth on the table.

"I can't believe you're still smoking. *Everybody's* quit."

"What's it going to do?" He lit up. "Kill me?"

"Ugh."

"Sorry. Gallows humor. It comes with the territory." He let out a long blue plume of smoke. "A sign of what?"

"What I'm supposed to be doing. Taking care of you. What do you think? You and me in Sarasota." It was an image so clear she could bite it: Harriet and Izzy, with her ministering to his needs, Lauren Bacall to his Bogart, Greer Garson to his Ronald Colman. She saw herself strolling him along the boardwalk, among the geeks and strongmen and bearded ladies, and the clowns in their stiff wigs.

"And you shouldn't be alone," she said.

"What makes you think I'd be alone?"

"What? Are you dating someone?"

He clutched his chest. "It's a Christmas miracle!" He was kidding. He stubbed out his cigarette, laughing. "I'm moving into a retirement community for old clowns. The circus is very generous. I get full disability. And the old clowns are kind of cool. Some of them go back to the thirties. Boxcar days."

"Sounds like fun. Take me with you."

"Oh, Har," he sighed.

She knew what was coming. Gay or straight, all men sounded the same when they were breaking it off.

"You're such a sweetheart," he said.

"Oh, God. Don't say that. All my life men have said that. Usually followed by *but*. You're such a sweetheart, but I need some space. You're such a sweetheart, but I got a job in Seattle. You're a peach, but I met an aerobics instructor named Daphne."

"You're a funny girl."

"Yeah, they say that too."

"If you haven't noticed, my dear, I'm *not* other men."

"But still you're leaving me."

"Only in the sense we all leave. Sooner or later."

When they were fifteen, and just about this time of year, they both got their first pairs of eyeglasses. Later they would graduate to contact lenses, but they were thrilled with the adultness of wearing glasses. They went out on the town, trying out their new look and feeling very cerebral. "Cary Grant in *Bringing Up Baby*," Harriet cried, so Izzy started talking like Cary Grant. They stood under the big tree at Rockefeller Center and discovered that, if they removed their glasses, the colored lights blurred magnificently. It was trippy. They stood for minutes, heads hung back, mouths open, dangling their new eyeglasses from their fingers. They felt sorry for anyone who wasn't nearsighted.

And now she pulled back and socked Izzy in the arm. "Fuck you," she said. "How could you?"

"Ouch. That hurts." He flinched.

She socked him again. "Who was it? Some clown groupie you balled between the elephant cages?" Her fist landed in the folds of his shirt. "A toothless carnie, maybe? Threw him down in the saw-dust? What did you do, screw the ringleader in top hat and tails?" She hit him again. "You're disgusting."

He cowered against the window, blocking her blows with his hands. "Stop it, will you? Cut it out."

"You didn't think about anyone else. You didn't even think about me. What am I supposed to do now? Why won't you let me take care of you?"

"Because! You're hurting me. You'd serve me dead rats like Bette Davis served Joan Crawford in *What Ever Happened to Baby Jane?*"

Harriet started crying. "See? You *know* that, Iz. What am I going to do when no one else knows *What Ever Happened to Baby Jane?*"

"You meet some new people. And it wouldn't hurt to see some newer movies."

"Well, here's the thing," she said. "Remember we once spent a whole Saturday going from movie theater to movie theater, and all the projectionists knew our names and comped us, and we saw Orson Welles walking down Eighth Street and that fat man at the restaurant in Little Italy treated us to a linguini dinner because we were such nice kids, and we were still eating our puttanesca when some gangster got his brains splattered all over the sidewalk right in front? Okay. Well, if that wasn't supposed to be the best day in our lives maybe you should have notified me or something, because it's still the best in *my* life." She cracked open a fortune cookie. "In the top five, anyway."

"It was a fine day, wasn't it?"

She dug her chin into his shoulder and she could feel his bone cut through the flannel. Izzy signaled for the check. He was a sly dog—he was officially ending this line of conversation—and like a brat Harriet wanted to persist. It took everything she had to stop talking.

They paid the check and went for a long walk in the streets, speaking very little. She dragged her hatbox behind them. On Sixth Avenue a men's choir sang "Sexual Healing" in three-part harmony. Some of the choristers had sunken eyes. A crowd of people gathered and threw coins and bills into an upended fedora. Harriet and Israel stopped briefly until the choir finished the song and received a scattered ovation, and then they started singing "Tainted Love" and Harriet's blood drained to her feet. They drifted by a Korean greengrocer with pyramids of fruit on the sidewalk, casting yellow and orange light into their faces. A Dominican in an apron sat on an orange crate, watching for shoplifters with one eye open like a cat. "Hey mister," he said, and pressed a tangerine into Izzy's hand. Harriet didn't know why. But things like that always happened to him. Panhandlers gave him single carnations, bouncers unlatched their velvet cordons, and vendors dropped extra falafel patties into his pita. Izzy thanked the Dominican, and as he peeled the tangerine a spray of juice burst from its skin. He handed her a crescent. The flavor flooded her mouth.

"This is," he said, his mouth full, "the best tangerine I've ever had. And I'm from Florida."

She would have to memorize all of this: the singing, the taste of tangerine and the seed he spit on the pavement, the fog his breath made. Someday she would need it. Holding his arm she glanced up to see, on top of the buildings, the black silhouettes of water towers, staved and coopered and quaint. She shivered.

"This city's full of ghosts," she said.

"Doesn't have to be."

The sky was a slate-colored ribbon over the avenue. But as she looked specks began to spiral out of the clouds like badminton birdies. It was snowing. Big flakes, each elaborate as a doily, landing on her nose and on the sidewalk, where they clung for a second before disappearing. A Japanese girl in a long maroon coat held her arms tight to her sides, scrunched her eyes shut, and stuck out her tongue; the two men she was with, a couple, started to laugh.

"Now you have to stay," Harriet said. "At least until the snow covers all the garbage. It's so pretty."

He took her hand and thrust it into the pocket of his army coat. It was a deep pocket and she could feel some items knocking around in there. A couple of tokens and a pack of cigarette papers. Neither of them wore gloves. Their hands were cold and spiny, and Izzy's felt so frail in hers she was afraid she might crush it. She wanted to believe they were simply wandering, the way they used to, with no particular destination, but she knew he was steering her some-where, tugging her around corners and nudging her across streets. Finally they were at the West Fourth Street subway stop and his pace slowed.

"This is where I get off, sweetie," he said.

"You're taking the subway? For God's sake, get a cab. I'll go with you."

"I like the subway," he said.

They stood shoulder to shoulder for a few minutes, watching a pickup game on the basketball court. Men dribbled and sprinted, rolling in unison from one end of the playground to the other. The snow fell on them, too. She pressed her fingertips against Izzy's knuckles. As they stood there three subways came and left; she could hear the screeching of brakes beneath them. The smell of hot metal came up through the grate, mingling with the smells of chestnuts and snow and diesel.

"Okay," he said. "Give us a hug."

As she held him the marquee lights of the drugstore across the street splintered into shards. Her fingers probed under his jacket, pulled the tail of his flannel shirt from his jeans, and dug into his dry skin. He was nothing but bones. But it was him, it was Izzy, smelling of wool and tobacco and greasepaint and Brut, and as long as she kept her arms around him she could keep him from disintegrating into dust.

"Don't let go," she said.

And of course, on cue, he drew away and held her at arm's length. She looked at the blurry sidewalk, and he said, "Come on. Let me see your face."

She bucked up. He wanted her to buck up. Then he said, "Hey. You used to be Norma Desmond. You used to be big."

"I am big. The pictures got small."

"There you go." He kissed her on the lips, and with impressive grace for someone so sick, he ran down the stairwell into the mouth of the subway, not turning, not even once, for a last look.

He died in April. One of those gorgeous days when a breeze comes in off the East River. Harriet got a call from Sarasota, from one of the old clowns. She liked to think of them in their polka-dot trousers and enormous Buster Browns, gathered around his sickbed with rubbery frowns painted on their faces.

"He's gone, dear."

She liked that he called her *dear*. She liked *him*, his voice soft and musical. She cupped the receiver. She had an apartment of her own, now. Nothing fancy. A studio on Avenue D. She worked in the welfare office. She enjoyed telling people she was a civil servant; the sound of it made her feel as if she should be wearing a jaunty tricornered hat.

"It was peaceful. He was at home."

She felt a pang of jealousy. "Was he—"

"In pain? You know how it is."

But she didn't. No one wanted her around for the final reel.

"And listen, dearie. He had a request of you."

Harriet perked up. Izzy left her a message. He wasn't quite gone yet.

"He asked that you tell the father."

"Me?" It wasn't the message she had hoped for.

"He was very specific. Harriet must inform the rabbi, he said."

She took the subway to Brooklyn. She wore a business suit and rectangular black glasses, early sixties Paula Prentiss, sober as the situation demanded. In Brooklyn the locust trees were beginning to leaf. The rabbi's secretary asked her to wait in his office, and Harriet sat on the leather sofa. She turned and kneeled on the cushion to look at the picture from Selma. There was a smudge across it, maybe something she or Izzy left when he practiced tumbles.

When she heard the door open she tried to jump to her feet. Her heart drummed. The rabbi walked in, took a look at her, said, "Oh, God," and walked out again. She sat and waited for what seemed like a long time, wondering if she should follow him. Then the door opened again.

"He's gone, then?"

Harriet nodded. He still had those aquiline features, sharper with age. He sat behind his enormous desk and heaved his shoulders like a big bird of prey puffing its wings.

The rabbi sighed heavily. He pressed his eyelids with his fingertips.

"When?"

"This morning."

His left arm in its blue jacket sleeve quivered. "I'll have to make arrangements," he said. "For the body." The shaking stopped. "What an indignity, for you to have to come tell me."

"I don't mind." Then she realized the rabbi meant it was an indignity for *him*.

"Who notified you?" he demanded.

"A colleague of his." An old clown.

"You two," he said, shaking his head. "Inseparable."

"We were, weren't we?" Harriet said, encouraged.

"Absolutely inseparable. I always thought it was unhealthy." He aimed his face at her. How many bar mitzvah boys must have quaked with fear on this very sofa? "Of course that was before I comprehended all the—"

His lips straightened into a flat bloodless line.

"All the implications," Harriet offered. Fathers and sons. What a mystery. In the silence she felt the shifting of tectonic plates.

"I assume he told you I was a bigot. Let me assure you, young lady. I am not a bigot. I counsel families in these matters. Sexuality and what have you."

"He never said you were a bigot."

"No? I'm surprised. He said it to me often enough."

His arm started to jerk violently. They both looked at it, as if a squirrel had scampered onto the desk.

"Anyway," she said, when the jerking subsided, "you don't have to make arrangements. Izzy's being cremated."

He lifted an eyebrow. "Of course he is." It was hard to understand how someone so chilly could share Israel's DNA, but he did, and Harriet found herself wanting to linger there. She figured if she stuck around long enough Israel's molecules might rise from the furniture and reconstitute themselves in the empty space.

"Yes, he specified cremation," she continued. "And the remains." Actually, Harriet wasn't sure about the remains. The old clown neglected to tell her. She scuttled for something to say. "They're going to shoot him out of a cannon."

"A cannon?"

"Not a real cannon. You know. One of those little toys in the circus." If his father understood him at all he would get it. "Clowns lighting the fuse. Instead of a boom it goes off with a pop, and Izzy's remains plop into the sawdust, with the elephant dung and the straw."

"Is that right?" The rabbi was smiling now, faintly. He was willing to play.

"Then the Shetlands and Clydesdales and pachyderms and dromedaries and all the animals walk around in a circle, gather their hooves on round little stanchions, and rear up and flash their mammaries in salute. An elegant tiger slinks into the ring with a lady tiger-tamer in fishnets snapping a whip. And all the freaks drift in from the sideshows: the pituitary cases, the fat, the hairy, the slithery, dwarves and giants, playing bugles and hoisting umbrellas. I mean, it's not exactly Talmudic, but it's festive."

"Indeed."

"Above it all the trapeze lady teeters on the rim of a platform." A platform with just a little bounce, like a diving board, and the same sandpaper tread, and still her footing is unsteady, the pink toes of her ballet slippers curling over the edge. She is long-waisted and agile and glittery, and she grabs the bar as it swings her way—one hand, two hands—and the platform falls away from her feet as she hurtles into the darkness. No net. Then her skin prickles in the sudden white spotlight, and from the opposite end of the tent the clown, in a red bulb nose and comical shoes and a crushed derby, flies toward her in a low nimble arc and catches her by the ankles just in time for her release.

INTO THE BLUE AGAIN

Lydia was at home in the ocean, suspended in the muscular curve of a barrel that charged the shore, her blood rising to match the surf. The best moment of the day was in the brisk dawn as she paddled, belly down, to the lineup; the greatest longing hit her four hours later, as she completed paperwork or processed a new guest in her windowless office and a plug of salt water dropped from her nostril and dampened her desk, infusing the room with the smell of marine life.

She was a teacher. An aerobics instructor but a teacher, still, and she knew that grace did not come easily to everybody. But when she shifted her weight on the board, negotiating the swells of the spring tide, she felt as if she were keeping her end of an evolutionary bargain: the return to the sea. She hoped to inspire this headiness in her adult students, as she cued up her mix tapes of Taylor Dayne and Laura Branigan, but what came so naturally to her—movement, balance, breath—was for them a strain, ugly and embarrassing.

She taught in the mirrored rooms of Bally's, but spent her spare time hanging out in the coffee shops and crab shacks of La Jolla, and it was in one of these, on a bulletin board jammed with announcements of boards for sale, yoga classes, and roommates wanted, that she found a flier inviting volunteers to pick coffee in Nicaragua. The foot of the leaflet was perforated into strips and each strip bore a phone number. Lydia plucked one, rolled it like a cookie fortune, and stuck it in her jeans pocket where it stayed for three days.

She called the number at the end of a particularly dull afternoon, and before she knew it, she was getting tropical inoculations.

When she told her parents she was going to Nicaragua, they said nothing. She had gotten bigger over the years, or they had gotten smaller, and they were bashful with her. She pulled the Rand-McNally globe from her old bedroom and twirled it until she found her destination. They ran their fingers over the ridges representing the Cordillera Isabelia as if they could derive meaning from them, like Braille.

The forty members of the Roberto Clemente (¡presente!) Brigade met in the Miami airport. It was February, and most of them were arriving from cold climates: Chicago, Boston, Brooklyn, St. Paul. Like a Lean Cuisine they were taken out of the freezer and slammed in the oven. Stepping out of the plane on the Managua runway, they thought they had stepped directly into the heat of the jets. But no, Nicaragua was *that* hot. Lydia was from California; she acclimated. In the first days of their orientation she rose early each morning in the Managua motel, ate pink and orange fruits, took notes on the meetings with representatives from the women's organizations and the labor unions, and observed how attractive all the Sandinistas were, including the women, smashing in their pressed fatigues and conch-colored nails. At night the *brigadistas* drank Victoria beer in a bar strung with colored lanterns, and Lydia, who had not mastered the difference between the FSLN and the FMLN, sat with Paco, the brigade leader, a philosophy graduate student from Columbia, and the other boys who argued about liberation theology, while some of the women snickered that she was from the wrong end of California, and that she was an aerobics instructor.

On their last night in Managua, before they were dispatched to the coffee region in the mountains to the north, they took a midnight swim at the motel. A troupe of Cuban ballerinas appeared on the patio and slithered into the pool, their sylph bodies barely disturbing the surface of the water. The North American women collected in the deep end and clung to the rim, flattening their legs against the concrete, except for Lydia, who paddled out to greet the dancers. "Lydia's skinny," one of the women said. "She can go talk to them."

She was the prototype of the Southern California girl: tall, sturdy, broad-shouldered. She gleamed with a surfeit of calcium. Strong hair and teeth. She turned out to be a good coffee picker, the third most productive member of the brigade after an Oregon woman from a lesbian logging commune and a software engineer from Cupertino who ran marathons. At the end of the day they dragged their sacks of coffee beans to the scale where Hipólito Esquinca, the plantation foreman, weighed them and marked the results on a board, and after the entire brigade had weighed in he tapped her as *Numero Tres*.

The revolution granted each farm a pig, and the Esquinca family, unpracticed in the arts of slaughter and butchery, adopted theirs as a family pet and named her Cecelia. She rooted through the uncooked rice in the kitchen, or endured the games of the migrant children who played in the clearing with sticks and flags. When Lydia patted the pig, she was surprised to feel her hide as coarse and prickly as a rhino's.

On Saturday they worked only half the day, and Lydia got the inspiration to walk into town. Tired as they were, she convinced her comrades the exercise would do them good, and dangled the possibility of buying candy in town, or hot sauce to enliven their diet of rice and beans. So a group banded, including Paco, who took his leadership responsibilities seriously and felt he should be a part of any expedition away from the farm. It was a mile and a half straight uphill to the village of Las Cruces, 110 degrees, and two o'clock by Paco's watch, which he had dutifully set to Central Standard Time when he left the Miami airport, but which seemed to bear no relationship to any chronological coordinates in Nicaragua.

The village smelled like burning rubber, as Managua had—a tinge of toxicity in the sinuses. At the center of town was a large hangar where farmers weighed and sold truckloads of coffee. Men in straw hats sat on the loading dock, watching the North Americans as they passed. A store with a red Coca-Cola sign was closed. That was a disappointment: in Managua warm bottled Coke was available everywhere.

In the center of Las Cruces was a hard patch of earth where they came upon a market—three or four rows of tables under droopy awnings and, in the aisles between them, women in thin dresses dawdling and fanning themselves, and children darting like pinballs. One of the stalls had a boom box that was playing "Hello." The brigadistas were dumbfounded by the national preoccupation with Lionel Richie. On the bus ride from Managua they met a group of soldiers with thin and boyish mustaches, and the brigade members tried to cajole the soldiers into singing patriotic songs of revolution. But the soldiers insisted on "Stuck on You."

"So uncool," Paco grumbled in the middle of the market.

Lydia shrugged. "I like Lionel Richie." When he looked at her she said, "I mean, some of his songs are okay." She swung her arms. "Get you moving."

Paco and the other men gravitated to a table that sold revolutionary tchotchkes: Sandino keychains and pennants, revolutionary armbands. They could not find chocolate but came across small bags of candied dots and the miniature boxes of Chiclets they had not seen since the Halloweens of their infancies.

An old woman was sitting behind a table covered with what looked like bladders: plastic bags bulging with black liquid, each bag tied with a twist tie.

Lydia lifted one of the bladders and felt its weight flop out of one palm and into the other. "*¿Qué es?*"

"Coca-Cola," the old woman replied.

She continued to shift the liquid between her hands. "*¿Cuánto?*"

"*Cuarenta centavos.*"

She reached into her jeans for change and when she was left holding the bag of soda she asked, "How do I drink it?"

The old woman shrugged, and a man's voice said, "You bite it."

She was startled to find herself looking up. Not many men in Nicaragua, even among the *internacionalistas*, were taller than she was. The man's face was curiously unlined, and his hair was pomaded to hold the grooves of his comb. He had a whiff of aftershave. Lydia's impulse was to laugh; he was a vintage idea of a ladies' man, shirt opened at the collar, and sunglasses raised to his forehead like a second pair of eyes.

"I am Eduardo Garcia Ortega y Mayor."

She said hello.

"And who might this be?" His accent was different from that of most Nicaraguans. He pronounced his sibilants.

"This? Me?" She felt her hand lifted in his, which was damp and unpleasant. "I'm Lydia. From La Jolla."

"Of course. A California girl. I wish they all could be California girls."

"You know La Jolla?"

"I was seven years in California. San Mateo. Beautiful place."

"Are you a Spaniard?" she asked.

He laughed: he bared his teeth, which were unnaturally white, and said, "Ha ha ha." Then his smile vanished and he said, "No. I am from here."

"I'm only asking because you're tall."

"Most people here suffer from malnourishment," he said. "Their growth is stunted."

Lydia nodded. They watched some children bait a mangy dog. Then she realized Paco was among them, wearing a red and black tricorn hat.

"We can grow and fish anything here," Eduardo continued, "but the Sandinistas are exporting our best food to Europe."

She nodded again. Then she registered what he said. "What?"

"You internacionalistas hear one side of the story. Someday you must hear the other side. The side of the true Nicaraguans. Do you believe in freedom?"

It felt like a trick question, like her high school history teacher asking who discovered America. "Uhh," Lydia said.

"I thought so," Eduardo said, more to himself than to her. He pointed to her bag of Coke. "You bite a hole in the corner and suck. See how the children do it." And he pointed to some really little kids who were suckling their baggies like teats. Then he looked at her. "Go ahead."

She did not want to bite and suck the bag in front of him. "I'm saving it for later."

"Your friends," he said, "they have a desire for Sandinista souvenirs."

She could spot them wandering the market in their red and black bandannas. "Sure. I guess."

"What is it you do in California?"

"I teach aerobics. I mean, that's what I'm doing now. It's kind of temporary, though, until I finish my degree in physical therapy. It's all right. I meet a lot of interesting people and I get to stay in shape while I work. Of course what I really like to do is surf."

His pupils contracted to a pair of pencil points. "You work with the body."

"I guess that's what I do."

"I might have known it."

She let the comment drop into the dry dirt between them. Lydia was used to compliments that sounded like insults.

"I am sure you pick more than your share of coffee," Eduardo said. "Most of the *norteamericanos* come here with heads full of ideas but bodies unequal to the task."

"No, I'm third," Lydia said. "Usually. They're pretty good on the brigade."

Eduardo looked toward the horizon, where a chemical haze settled close to the ground. "The brigade. The brigade." He seemed to be remembering an old song. He asked, "Which plantation are you working?"

"The Esquinca farm." Lydia lifted her bag of soda and indicated the direction from which they had trudged. "That way."

He turned to look, although there was nothing to see but trucks pulling up to the warehouse. It occurred to her then maybe she was not supposed to reveal their residence. He lifted her free hand, and for a nauseating moment she was afraid he was going to kiss it. If he did she would break out into giggles, a bad habit of hers when she was nervous or embarrassed. But he only squeezed it, shifting her bones between his fingers as if he were testing veal for tenderness. "If you tire of rice and beans," he said, "you may visit me. I live west of town. It is the only stone house on the road toward the ocean."

She felt as far from the ocean as Mars.

"Sure. Okay."

At bedtime they unrolled their sleeping bags over the small mounds of green coffee beans spread around the mill to dry. The sleeping arrangement was Lydia's idea, after a single night in the barracks where they were assigned to sleep on shelves like jars of mustard. Most of the brigade spent that night awake, listening to the crying of the babies and staring at the single bulb that burned until daybreak, and suspicious of the old man coughing whom one of the nurses said had tuberculosis.

But the hills of coffee were as cozy as a beanbag, as the brigadistas curled in their sleeping bags and looked up at the sharp constellations. Paco, still wearing his glasses, sighed and said, "We were supposed to be living with the people."

"Oh, well," Lydia said. "I think the people are glad we're out here."

Cecelia the pig walked by their feet and stood like an attentive hound, her bulk a dark silhouette against the less-dark sky.

"Who was that guy at the market?" Paco asked.

"Guy?" Lydia said.

"The Ricardo Montalban guy."

"Some guy from town."

"Was he putting the moves on you?"

"I don't know what he was doing," Lydia said. "I think he was what you call, you know. A contra."

Paco sat up in his sleeping bag. "What makes you say that?"

"Oh, I don't know." Lydia tried to act casual but she was humbled by the gravity of her own words. "This and that. Stuff about freedom and the people."

"That sounds like the Sandinistas to me," the software engineer said from two bags down.

"Yeah, but different," Lydia said. "The words were the same but it came out sounding like the opposite."

Paco lay down and stared at the sky. "Did he ask you questions?"

"A couple."

"Did he ask who was on the brigade?"

"He saw us. But I didn't give him any names." She patted the quilting of her bag. "I told him where we're working. I guess that was wrong."

The migrant worker on defense detail, his rifle on his shoulder, strolled by on his rounds, pausing briefly to make sure they were safe.

Paco adjusted his glasses. "That's okay," he said.

In the morning Paco gave a little pep talk that ended, as always, "*¿Ahora qué?*" To which the brigade all shouted, "*¡A cortar café!*" They spent the day in the jungle, each in a cocoon of green leaves dotted with red coffee beans, hearing each other but not seeing each other. One of the boys would chant, "You may find yourself in another part of the world."

To which someone else would answer: "Living in a shotgun shack."

"You may ask yourself . . ."

"My God! What have I done?"

Early in the brigade's second week, when everyone's muscles throbbed and they were all beginning to lose weight, Wolfe appeared. Just Wolfe: he did not bother with patronyms. How he found them no one knew. Wolfe had been kicking around Nicaragua for six months or so, depending on whom you asked. He told someone he was from Chicago and someone else he came from Seattle. No one pinned him down to a consistent story or to a conversation that lasted more than a few seconds. Paco grumbled that Wolfe was a revolution whore, one of the norteamericanos who loved the romance of rebellion but, too undisciplined to stick to a single assignment, floated from brigade to brigade, town to town.

Wolfe played the guitar. He wore striped parachute pants, even into the jungle to cut coffee, which he did well. His Spanish, which he said he'd picked up since arriving in Nicaragua, was uneven. The accent was terrible but his vocabulary was wide and surprising. He knew the words for *colander* and *cistern*. If Paco were concerned that Wolfe would disrupt the sexual ecology of the group, he needn't have worried; Wolfe was affectionate with men and women alike, more like a child than a predator.

Then one morning they woke up wishing they were dead. Not all of them—just an unlucky half. Diarrhea they were used to; this was something else. This was like being knifed up the belly and inverted like a mango. The two outhouses were occupied so they crawled into the jungle, squatted, and sweated, excreting everything they had eaten, and then pieces of intestine, sloughed-off cells, and acid shards of stomach. Wolfe, healthy and cheery, walked around dispensing toilet paper from a roll he had pinched at the Managua airport.

The nurses administered Pepto-Bismol. Then the nurses got sick. They guessed a contaminant in the water source had overpowered their purification tablets. Still, they drank water to prevent dehydration.

Lydia did not get sick. But she lay awake at night, reclining on the coffee beans and listening to the groans around her, wondering if somehow she had brought this on, if Eduardo had poisoned the well.

On the third morning of the sickness, Paco crawled out of his sleeping bag and said, "I'm dying." Lydia walked behind the mill and found Wolfe packing his duffel bag.

"You're *leaving*?" she said, careful to modulate the desperation in her voice.

"The brigade's got some bad mojo," he said. "Besides, I met this *chica* on the Transportation Ministry I want to go see."

When Wolfe walked out of the compound, the migrant children clung to his arms and legs and then fell off him one by one. Cecelia and Lydia followed him to the edge of the clearing and watched him disappear into the forest.

Bodies were strewn throughout the plantation like some medieval portrait of hell. When Wolfe wandered away she knew she was alone.

She found Paco crouching under some branches, his pants around his ankles and shirt covering his privates, a wad of paper in his hand. "Go away, I'm naked," he said.

"Sick naked doesn't count. Besides, I'm studying to be a physical therapist, which is kind of like a doctor. I mean, we take anatomy, but we don't have to take organic chem and all that stuff."

Paco pressed his damp forehead against his knee. "So humiliating."

"It's not so bad. Chemistry was never my strong point."

"I mean me."

"Oh. I know." She crouched beside him and placed her hand on the back of his neck.

"That feels good."

"The laying on of hands. It's the best." She felt the knob of his vertebra, startlingly prominent. "I'm worried about the sickness."

"It's just Montezuma's revenge. Or Sandino's revenge."

"I did spring break in Cabo. This is not Montezuma's revenge."

Paco shrugged, she thought, but it was kind of a shudder too. He understood the seriousness of the predicament.

"Isn't there someone in Managua we can call for help? Someone who organizes the brigades?"

"I have a number, but"—he lifted his face—"we don't have a telephone. And I don't know how to use the phones here anyway. What sounds like a busy signal is a dial tone. What sounds like a dial tone is a phone ringing. Nothing here makes sense." He buried his face in his knees. "We have nurses. We're supposed to take care of ourselves."

"The nurses have passed out."

"We were supposed to be living among the people."

"Yeah. I know. But right now we're shitting on the coffee bushes and I don't think we're doing the people much good. Look," she said, "I'm still feeling pretty good. So I was thinking maybe I should go see that guy Eduardo."

"Who?"

"The guy from town."

"The lounge lizard?"

"Why not?"

Paco groaned. "Because he's a sleazebag, at best. And at worst he's some kind of counterrevolutionary."

"He used to live in California."

"It's too dangerous."

Lydia stood up and slapped the dust from her jeans. She had been told this before: going off to school, driving into San Diego, surfing, traveling—all of it someone or other had cautioned her against. After weigh-in, with only three brigadistas left standing, she headed up the hill, against the gathering darkness.

The village was bald and deserted. A corrugated garage door was padlocked at the coffee warehouse. The fair was gone. Only some litter and a couple of rough-looking dogs nosing through the dirt indicated that it was a place of commerce. Of the four roads heading out of town, none seemed to go in the direction of the last haze of day, so she had to guess which way was west, toward the sea. She could smell people's suppers cooking, beans and meats, and she remembered she had skipped her dinner. She passed a few low cement houses. From some she heard a radio playing accordion music or European pop. She remembered with a sudden stab of homesickness a boyfriend at home who loved the Ramones, and who danced by jumping up and down in one spot, his arms motionless as fins.

The houses began to thin out as she walked. She was sure she had not seen a stone house and began to wonder if she had taken the wrong road. Once it became seriously dark she might have to appeal to a family for help, with her bad Spanish: find a place to stay for the night. Wolfe had done as much in his travels, he said. The revolution had made everyone hospitable, especially toward the internacionalistas. It was different for a boy, though.

Then the houses came to an end. She passed a couple of businesses—a mechanic, a dentist—that were closed and blank. Ahead she saw the malevolent curve of a dog's back as he sniffed the ground. A truck passed her on the road, nearly grazing her with its side mirror, and the dog ran off as the truck barreled through. She proceeded.

A few yards ahead she saw a light. As she neared it she saw more lights, winking behind tree branches, and heard a hum that she thought was distant traffic but that grew, steadily and discernibly, to be "Thriller." Vincent Price laughed just as she reached the house. Stone, yes, and surrounded by a stone fence four feet high, the top of which was embedded with colorful splinters of glass. There was an iron gate, which she entered cautiously. The music was so loud she might not hear a dog rushing toward her, leaping on her as it bared its black gums. She followed a flagstone path through some cacti and came to a front door painted blue with a knocker that looked, to her, like a prop from a play. She lifted it and banged.

The music continued. She banged harder, persistently, until the record cut off, midphrase, and she knocked again, a little more quietly this time, but firmly, to be heard.

When the door opened Eduardo, sweaty and winded, blinked into the darkness. "Yes?"

"Hi. You said I could come by."

He was naked. At least from the waist up—Lydia kept her eyes fixed on his face, so she wasn't sure about the rest of him. Besides, he hid most of his body behind the door. Apparently he had been having sex; he had been having sex and she couldn't be more unwelcome.

"And you are?"

"Lydia. Remember? We met in the market last week. From California."

His face clouded. Then recognition broke over him, and he assumed his continental demeanor. "Of course! Lydia from California. The exercise instructor."

"I'm actually studying to be a physical therapist."

"And I have been exercising. It must be fate. Come in, please!"

He backed up and she, careful not to lower her eyes, followed him. His home was spacious and clean, with a whitewashed dining room that opened out to a lush courtyard dense with banana trees. The area was dominated by a teak dining table surrounded by heavy, ornately carved chairs, straight-backed and uninviting. Someone's idea of elegance.

"Please, sit down," he said, pulling a chair out for her. He was not naked per se; he wore a pair of briefs, electric blue with white piping. But the briefs were so short and snug he might as well have been nude. He also wore a pair of Adidas and socks. She sat and was startled by a caw. A parrot perched in the courtyard. "Can I pour you some rum?" He stood in the adjoining kitchenette, holding a bottle high for her to see.

"No thank you."

He still held the bottle, insisting. She said nothing.

"Some water then."

"No, no water."

"Don't worry. It's bottled. I am sure you are thirsty." She listened to the glugging of water from a bottle and willed her muscles to relax. He served her in one of those heavy blown glasses with a blue rim—they were common in La Jolla households—and said, "Allow me to wash and dress. Please, Lydia, be comfortable."

While he was gone she looked into the courtyard and then moved to the fancy tape deck, the only other furniture in the room. She sipped the water skeptically. Water was poison.

When Eduardo returned he looked like the man she had met in the market, freshly combed and splashed, in chinos and a powder blue shirt and a delicate gold chain. Even though she had refused the rum, he poured them each a glass.

"Nicaraguan rum used to be the finest in the world," he said. "Something else your Sandinistas have destroyed. Now it is undrinkable. As bad as Cuban." He showed her the label. "I am reduced to drinking Puerto Rican."

One glass would not make her drunk, and she decided it would be best for her and her comrades to be sociable with him. She was a spy on a mission. James Bond always drank. "All rum tastes the same to me," she said.

"But you are so wrong."

She sat at the table and nursed her rum, while he leaned against the arch leading into the kitchen. "Do you know a doctor?" she asked.

He looked at her for a second, then contorted his face into concern. "You are ill?"

"No, I'm fine. It's the other brigadistas. They're all sick."

"Of course. You are stronger than they."

"I've been lucky."

"Nonsense. You treat your body with respect. These others, they feed on romantic ideals. It makes them weak."

"I think it may be the water. We've been purifying it, but—"

"Tourists' disease."

"No. This is something else. Turista passes in a day or so. This thing lingers."

He held the bridge of his nose. "For how long does it linger?"

"Days. Four or five days and no one's getting any better. They need a doctor."

"Dysentery." He nodded conclusively. "It's from the animals in the water."

"Animals? Like pigs?"

"Small animals."

"Mice?"

He sighed. "I do not know the name in English. The very small animals that have no shape." With his fingers he illustrated expansion and contraction, like a jellyfish.

"Oh. Amoebas."

"Amoebas, yes."

A friend of Lydia's got amoebas in India. She was sick for six months.

"You must be hungry."

She was starving, but knew she had to press on. "So, do you know a doctor?" Her voice quavered. What was she doing here? Separated from her friends, with a man she knew nothing about? She had no choice but to press.

"There is a doctor, yes. Not in Las Cruces but in Matagalpa. It's thirty kilometers away. He comes here the first Wednesday of each month."

Lydia had lost track of dates since they had been in Nicaragua.

"Three weeks from now," Eduardo said.

"Three weeks!"

"Of course we can call him. For our international guests I am sure he will make a special trip."

She half-stood. "So let's call."

"Ah, but we can't. Not until the morning. Among other things the Sandinistas have rationed phone service. We won't be able to call until morning."

Lydia sat down and rubbed her eyes with the heels of her hands. She had come for nothing and had to walk home in the dark— preferable to accepting a ride from this creep. "Sorry to have bothered you."

"No. You must stay the night. In the morning we will call and then we will fetch the doctor. I have a car."

She stared at the rum she'd barely touched. So that was his game. But she wasn't that kind of a spy. And even the queasiest member of the brigade would not expect her to barter herself in exchange for some medical care.

Eduardo laughed. He seemed to have learned his laugh from the "Thriller" record. "You misunderstand me. You will have your own room."

This he had learned too. Probably from one of those creepy movies from the sixties in which the girl gets adorably drunk and passes out in a man's bed while he spends a fitful and gentlemanly night on the couch. Lydia used to watch them on TV when she was little. "I'm sorry." She pushed the glass away. "I was wrong to come. I better go."

"Go back to your supper of rice and beans and your bad water? Don't be laughable." Eduardo took away the glass of rum, which Lydia interpreted as a sign of good faith, and decanted it back into the bottle. "Let me show you the house."

She studied the front door, heavy and pompous as the dining set. She worked in public places and was used to designing an exit plan. She was also used to deflecting men's advances; after all, she worked with bodies, molding them and punishing them, and there was an intimacy in her labors that some unimaginative men read as sexual. She had learned to use her authority: a simple "Now, then!" could put the most arrogant of office-supply salesmen in his place.

"I do not bite," he said.

They walked through the courtyard, which was crisscrossed with shadows. On the opposite side they came to a room like a cell, with a single high window set deep in a niche. Only it was a cell cluttered with junk: barbells, trophies, a desk stacked with files and magazines and an eight-by-ten photo of Eduardo, standing with another guy who had the same anchorman haircut and a uniform. A mirror with a gold-leaf frame dominated the wall above the desk. Eduardo picked up the picture and looked at it fondly. Then he handed it to Lydia so she could read the inscription: "To Eddie, For All Your Help. Ollie."

"Colonel North," he said.

She handed it back to him.

"Like me, a man with a passion for life. Fine cigars, beautiful boats, beautiful women. Have you seen his secretary? She reminds me of you."

Lydia was unimpressed. Cigars and boats meant nothing to her, and men who boasted that they loved women actually didn't. Her own preference tilted toward the surfer dudes she ran with in La Jolla, boys with easy laughs and yarn bracelets who strolled the hot sidewalks barefooted, and who demanded as little of her as they did of themselves. The photograph made her nauseous. "What sort of work did you say you do?"

"Import export." He took the frame from her and adjusted it on the desktop. He was standing close enough to graze her hip. She leaned away. There was nowhere to step. Her legs were drained of blood.

Eduardo's attention was caught by his reflection in the mirror, and she looked too. A glum California girl and a well-groomed dandy. It was as though their pictures had been cut out of two different magazines and taped side by side.

"We are two specimens," he said. He was staring, not at her image but at his own. "You and me. Examples of a superior race."

"I don't know about that."

"But of course you are being modest. You have remained healthy while those about you fell prey to a parasite. People like us become objects of envy, of petty jealousy."

Poor guy! He believed this crap. It was the kind of schoolboy Nietzsche the Young Republicans were always spouting from their lonely little tables at the Student Activity Fair.

Without taking his eyes from the mirror Eduardo unbuttoned his shirt, languorously, seducing himself in a slow strip tease. Lydia found herself unable to look away. She was familiar with narcissism, but she couldn't recall ever having seen such a naked case. "When I lived in San Francisco I was a god," he said. "I had a trainer, an excellent man. A homosexual but nevertheless. Since my return I have lost definition. Here." He cupped his pectorals as if they were milk-bearing breasts. "And here." He stroked his bicep. "I believe you have come into my life for a reason."

"To procreate a superior race?" Lydia joked.

He looked at her sternly. "You misunderstand me."

She understood. He didn't want a lover. He wanted a trainer.

She shook her head. "We need a doctor. Now."

He looked at her sharply. In the mirror she saw his head jerk around. He was not a man used to being denied, or at least that was what he wanted her to believe. She was suddenly tired, so tired she wanted to find a spot on the crowded floor where she could curl up and go to sleep. From a distance she heard the screech of a cat, and from somewhere closer a generator hummed. She remembered learning that when the undertow drags you to the bottom, pummeling your board on top of you with the finality of a trapdoor snapping shut, every neuron in you fires the order to surrender. The trick, of course, is not giving in, but watching which way the bubbles rise and following them to the breakers.

"A doctor," she said. "Tonight. Tomorrow we begin training."

They traveled by his Jeep over the rutted road, slowing here and there for a pig or a truck full of coffee. He had a tape deck, and he played "Thriller" loud enough that she felt no burden to talk. There were no lights along the road, just his headlights and more stars than she knew, and as they kept heading west, she began to smell the ocean pouring into the Bay of Fonseca.

STAGGERED MATURITIES

If you have ever had an obsession you know how it will expand like foam to fill the contours of your day. And if you are lucky enough to share that obsession, you understand that it creates an intimacy as intense as kissing. So when Vivian and Roberto found themselves in a sushi restaurant in Little Tokyo, plucking pieces of sashimi they could not afford from little boats floating down a tiny channel, she saw the adventure as a celebration of their friendship and not their insanity.

They were looking for Thor Hjelstrom, who read the evening financial report on the radio. Roberto described Thor's voice as "California sunshine, roughened by sand and sea salt." Roberto was from the Midwest. He was a native English speaker but had second-language tics, like starting sentences with "But" apropos of nothing. If Vivian said, "Let's go to lunch," Roberto would answer, "But let's eat at Subway." Sometimes he phoned her in the afternoon to say, "But how will Thor describe the Dow tonight?" This habit of his kept her off-kilter, as if she were engaged in a cosmic argument she couldn't understand.

Thor Hjelstrom had poetry in his soul. Credit default swaps, mezzanine debts, depository trusts, all music from the back of his throat. The worse the news the better he sounded. Vivian and Roberto chewed their sushi listening for the unmistakable rust of his voice. He had mentioned this very restaurant in one of his reports, joking that it was his stimulus contribution to stop there after work.

"Maybe if we throw some financial terms around he'll find us," Vivian suggested.

Roberto agreed. "Have some of my collateralized debt bonds," he said, waving his chopsticks like antennae.

"No thanks. I have cramdown effect."

Vivian knew Roberto from work. They typed closed-captions for television programs. When she applied for the job, she told them she was fluent in Tagalog, which wasn't exactly true—her Tagalog related mostly to family things, not to things on television, so while she knew how to say *gift wrap* she had no idea how to say *defibrillator*. But it turned out she didn't need Tagalog. She simply tapped out dialogue in shorthand that someone would translate overseas. Some of her co-workers liked to slip in mistakes just to see if they would get caught. So a Gossip Girl might explain that workers and farmers must struggle to expropriate the means of their production, or the Korean guy from *Lost* might confess he dreamed of being walked on by men wearing stilettos.

"But what a good girl you are," Roberto said when they first met. "Typing away in your cubicle. Don't tell me. Strict father, demanding mother, three hours of piano practice every night, and perfect SAT scores."

Vivian knew that men found comfort in this racial stereotype, and she did nothing to disabuse him. In fact, her father was a drunk. A sweet drunk, but a drunk nonetheless. He was the guy you found at closing time, weeping and singing along with Earth, Wind and Fire.

Their co-worker Julie was the first to go. She was called into the supervisor's office, and then she packed the pictures of her cats in a Suntory liquor carton. Julie never fooled around with her captions. The supervisor told her she underperformed.

Then came Justin, whom everyone liked because he could always produce free Clippers tickets. When he disappeared, the sabotage increased. Felicia began substituting large chunks of *Grey's Anatomy* with the manifesto of the Tamil Tigers. Heinrik encoded Tupac lyrics in an episode of *Ghost Whisperer*. Vivian stuck to her script, not out of loyalty but from lack of imagination.

Vivian and Roberto went to Malibu, where Thor Hjelstrom was known to surf. It was a chilly afternoon and the surfers cast long shadows on the beach as they emerged from the ocean in their wetsuits. Any one of them might have been Thor Hjelstrom—tall, chiseled, fortyish, with blond hair faded to oatmeal. "I want Thor Hjelstrom to put his arms around me," Roberto said. "I want him to protect my troubled assets. I want him to iron out the convolutions in my brain with his strong Viking hands."

Vivian nodded. She worried she was too shallow for him. For both of them—Roberto and Thor Hjelstrom.

When Roberto got fired, he decided to go back to Illinois. Vivian went to his apartment for the last time. They pulled the covers up to their chins and watched his favorite movie, *The World of Henry Orient*. It was about two girls running around New York wearing coolie hats and making slant eyes. "But it is a little racist," Roberto said in response to Vivian's silence. "You have to understand the time it was made."

"Okay," she said. She envisioned her and Roberto running around the city in coolie hats like two little girls. When the supervisor called her into his office, it was not to fire her but to tell her she would be taking on more responsibility. Vivian returned to her cubicle to caption *Two and a Half Men*. "What we need is capital market efficiency," Charlie Sheen said. "The accrued market discount has compromised our negative yield curve for the Macauley duration."

At the end of the day she packed her things in the trunk of her Toyota and tuned in Thor's voice. There were two skies over Los Angeles. To the south the sun flattened the shadows out of the city from Crenshaw down to Harbor Gateway, bearing heavy on the aftermarket auto-parts stores and wig shops that sold real Indian hair. To the north, steel-colored clouds hung low like awnings full of water over the San Gabriels, and Highway 2 cut sharp and deep like a canal dividing the cerebral hemispheres. She drove toward the rain.

STAND UP, SCOUT

Paper on pallets, freshly printed cutoffs, crosshatched and shrink-wrapped, lifted on the prongs of forklifts and loaded on trucks. Paper shreds in canvas gurneys. Paper in rolls like giant wheels of cheese. Butts of paper, too small for commercial printing, left out on the curb for butchers and art teachers to carry off under their arms. Maybe after the attacks the work slowed, but now, a few years later, the printers were recouping their losses: every investment house in lower Manhattan was rushing out a prospectus or a shareholders' report, and the narrow cow-path streets were choked with the scrimmage of business. When a good wind blew, the autumn air filled with paper like snow.

Penelope dressed like the traders and stock analysts: she studied how they looked and talked. On the street, dodging the hand trucks and dumpsters, she might have been mistaken for one of them. But when she returned from a quick lunch to her place of employment, she did not walk through a marble lobby, past a security guard and a sign-in book. She entered a dented metal door without so much as a sign or a window to distinguish it, so corroded and smoke-stained it blended into the brickwork; if a passerby bothered to notice the door, he might think it led to a boiler room or an obsolete coal cellar. That's the secret of lower Manhattan—there's manufacturing going on all over the place, a shadow economy that runs below the financial district like a subterranean river of ink. Once at a party she told a woman that she worked in a print shop on Vesey, and the woman said, without irony, "I didn't know those places still existed."

After she shoved the metal door open, she could hear the thumping of the web press, the shouting of the press operators, the rhythmic chomp of the three-knife guillotine. Paper. She loved the smell of it, the feel of it in her hand—she could tell you blindfolded if you gave her a forty-pound vellum or a forty-eight-gram news-print. She had to cross the factory floor to reach the office, which she shared with three other customer-service reps, two salesmen, a receptionist, and a human-resources specialist. It was cordoned off from the pressroom by glass and Sheetrock and insulation, and the insulation did a surprisingly good job of keeping out the noise. Every time an operator came in for a press check or to ask the HR specialist about his benefits, Penelope and the other office workers had to yell, "Shut the door!" so the thrum of the press wouldn't drive them crazy.

Ernie, the male receptionist—and that was *his* designation, not theirs; he greeted customers with "I'm Ernie, the male reception-ist"—pushed himself from his desk when he saw Penelope. "We just got a call from Miller-MacDonald. Rush job. They printed half a million forecasts with some bargain-basement printer before they caught a typo. Now they need the whole run reprinted by four tomorrow morning."

"Who did they go to with the original job?" Penelope asked.

"They didn't say."

"That's dandy. When are these people going to learn you get what you pay for?" But she was pleased. An emergency like this and she could charge whatever she wanted. Even with overtime costs they'd make a fortune. She called the client and named her price, upholding enough professionalism not to point out what happens when you try to save money by going to a cut-rate printer. Then she went out to talk to the press foreman about sending half the crew home so they could rest up and come in to work the overnight shift. When she got back to the office, Ernie was sulking. She could tell by the slope of his shoulders.

"Hey, this is good news," she said.

"I know. It's just that *my* job is the one getting pushed aside." Er-nie was trying to build a client base of his own. "It's a new account. No big deal or anything. Just a print broker. But it's our first job with him so I wanted it to be on time."

"Do you want me to talk to him?"

Ernie shrugged and turned away. "I don't know if it's such a good idea. He's Orthodox."

"I'm good with the Orthodox."

"I don't think they care for women in the industry."

"Nonsense. They're shrewd businessmen and do what they have to. Besides," she added, swiveling in her chair, "I'm a good bat mitzvah girl myself. I can always play that card."

"You are not," Ernie said.

She raised her hand in a pledge. "Scout's honor. What's the client's name?"

Ernie opened his drawer and picked a business card from the pencil tray. When Penelope took it, she said, "I know him."

"Get out."

"I do. I know him." She dropped the card in her purse. "I'll go over there."

"He's all the way in Brooklyn."

"It'll make a good impression. I'll go over there."

Penelope's bat mitzvah almost didn't happen. It was the result of a long, complex, contentious negotiation between her mother and her father. From upstairs she could hear them arguing, her mother's machine-gun voice, hardly stopping for a breath, and her father's exhausted interjections.

"Why should we capitulate to some medieval rite of passage to satisfy the expectations of people we hardly know?"

"What do you mean, hardly know?" her father answered. "They're our family."

"Your family. Not mine, Stuart."

"And Penelope's."

"So a rabbi says a few words and poof, she's a woman? That's so paternalistic. Did it ever occur to you she becomes a woman on her own? Through *her* experiences?"

"All right already."

"This is so typical of organized religion. You need a man to stand up and tell you when it's okay to move to the next phase of life."

"It doesn't mean anything to us. It means something to them. I thought it would be a small price to pay."

"And then what? Gift certificates? Jewelry? What kind of values are we teaching her?"

"We can ask for contributions to charity."

"*Charity?*"

"Forget it."

"What are we now, noblesse oblige?"

"I said forget it."

A few minutes later her mother was sitting on Penelope's bed, explaining what to expect on her bat mitzvah. That's the way it was with Mother. Usually she ended up conceding, but only after a good fight. Fighting was her oxygen. Penelope's mother was not at Woodstock. That's the way she put it: "I was *not* at Woodstock, Penelope." She might have been; she was the right age, and she had friends who were there. But Mother sniffed that Woodstock was nothing more than unserious people taking hallucinogens and listening to bands—some of which had talent, she'd allow—deliver substandard performances. Women were on their backs in the mud—"on their *backs*," she stressed—while Mother remained in the hot city, cranking fliers out of an old Gestetner mimeograph for a rally to legalize abortion.

"It just shows how superficial your generation is that you hold Woodstock up as some romantic emblem of the counterculture."

Penelope shrugged at this point, not aware that she held Woodstock up as anything.

"It had all of the depravity and none of the politics."

Once Mother acquiesced to the idea of the bat mitzvah, the three of them sat at the kitchen table to make plans. Penelope would not read from the Torah. She didn't speak Hebrew, and even if she learned enough to fake it, like the other thirteen-year-olds did, it would be an act of hypocrisy to recite the teachings of an ancient (and deeply sexist) spiritual text. Instead, Penelope would take on a research project under the direction of Rabbi Pearlman (who was Reformed, and a good man, for a rabbi—an old antiwar activist) and deliver a short talk to the congregation.

"It can be very creative," Mother said, now warm to the idea. She was very touchy when it came to her husband's family. She always suspected they hated her. Hated that she kept her own name, hated that she wanted only one child, hated that she was uninterested in synagogue or Hadassah. Before every family event she was nervous for days, and her nervousness took the form of bolstered militancy. She perceived misogyny everywhere, even on the *The Cosby Show*. "They both work, right? So how come she's always unpacking the groceries? Why can't his ass unpack the groceries?"

Then came the gathering, during which Mother would remain cool and silent. Penelope could not understand how her mother picked up on so much hostility; the grandparents, uncles and aunts, and many cousins on her father's side were always pleasant enough. And after the visit she endured the stages of Mother's grief: sniping on the car ride home ("I can't believe your cousin Denise is pregnant again. What is she, a cow?"); followed by a tantrum once they reached the house ("One question— they can't ask one question about how *I'm* doing? Would it kill them?"); followed, the next day, by a period of depression ("Am I a monster? Am I such a monster that they want to *shun* me?"), followed, a couple of days later, by penitence ("Denise! It's Vera, Stuart's wife. Listen, I need your address so I can send a little gift for the baby").

Penelope learned early there was no comforting Mother. If she tried to commiserate, saying something like, "Yeah, they're pretty old-fashioned," Mother would snap, "Since when are you so judgmental, missy?" If she tried to reason with her, saying, "They didn't really say anything mean," Mother would accuse her of being on "their side." Better to stay quiet.

Still, when she was riding high, Mother was better company than anyone. On Penelope's favorite days they took a field trip to Greenwich Village, where they revisited Mother's youth, and Penelope learned exactly where the Stonewall riots began and where Dylan was photographed with his girlfriend for the cover of *Freewheelin'*. These visits would end up at the Le Figaro Café where Penelope, feeling very grown-up, would drink a hot chocolate sprinkled with cinnamon while mother had a cappuccino and told Penelope about her favorite movies.

"*Breathless* was a revelation. Jean Seberg with that haircut. I wanted to be just like her, with that androgynous sexuality, you know?"

Penelope nodded, unsure what *androgynous* meant.

"Poor Jean! She tried to speak truth to power. Nice girls don't do that. But we're not nice girls, you and I. Are we, Penelope?"

"No."

"Because we speak truth to power. Even when it's unpopular. The rewards are few, but they are deep. Like Atticus Finch, when he walks out of the courtroom. Remember?"

In fact, Penelope had not yet seen the movie or read the book. But her mother had described the scene so many times and in such detail, she felt as if she had. *Stand up, Scout. Your father's passing.*

"Stand up, Scout." Mother shivered. "That gets me every time."

When Penelope began to prepare for her bat mitzvah, she had decided to research the Holocaust. But she got sidetracked by the TV news, footage of boys and girls throwing stones at Israeli tanks. The tanks swiveled their gun turrets, faceless like robots. Penelope was rooting for the children.

"How's your research coming on the Holocaust?" Mother asked.

"Actually, I decided to do something else. I'm going to talk about the establishment of Israel."

"Israel?" Her mother compressed her lips.

"I thought it would be more relevant."

"The Holocaust is always relevant."

"Rabbi Pearlstein said this would be good, too."

"Oh. Well. If you and the *rabbi* have discussed it."

"Don't worry, Mother. I won't disappoint you."

Penelope was free to concentrate on her research while Mother arranged everything else. The reception would be catered by a friend of Mother's. The guests would consist mostly of Dad's family. Mother's family, resolutely secular, thought the whole thing was a bad idea, so she didn't invite them. She asked Penelope if she wanted to have any friends from school, but Penelope didn't; this was a family event. Besides, Penelope was too busy to issue invitations, since she had two papers to write: one that she would give to Rabbi Pearlstein for his approval; and the real one, which she would read during the actual service. It was a guerrilla action, planned with precision. At night she paced her room, practicing her talk, picturing the ruckus it would cause when she told the truth, and how she would emerge, battle-scarred but saintly. A Jewish Joan of Arc.

The morning of the service they woke up early to get ready. Penelope wore a red dress. Her mother, in exceptionally good spirits, put on makeup and perfume. As Penelope watched her at the bathroom mirror, Mother said, "How about a little sparkle?" And Penelope closed her eyes with pleasure as Mother applied gold eye shadow, first on the left lid, then the right, with her gentle thumb.

The synagogue lobby was already buzzing by the time they got there, and Penelope suddenly understood why girls pine for their bat mitzvah. All these people—to see her. They all wore their best clothes and brought boxes wrapped in gold from Tiffany and Godiva and Macy's and piled them on top of a glass table with a huge lilac-colored vase. Penelope wanted to head straight for the presents, but she restrained herself. She knew what the protocol was. And all the introductions—there was Uncle Ira who pinched her cheek, hard; and Second Cousin Ramona with hair as stiff as ironwork; and Great Aunt Sadie with her big brown eyes that seemed to be filled with tears, but they were just rheumy. There was Cousin Zach with MS who zipped around in a motorized wheelchair and at one point crashed into the table, nearly upsetting the huge vase, as a general cry went up from the crowd. Aunt Celia ushered three boys: Ethan, Daniel, and Yael. "You remember? You and Yael used to play together?"

She did remember, once, somewhat sickeningly, being thrown together when they were about four, and running up to her room and pretending they were married. Now Yael was a thick boy with a round face and freckles.

Aunt Celia kissed her and immediately took out a tissue to wipe off the lipstick.

Mazel tov! Mazel tov! Such a blessed day. So many well-wishers. Penelope began to have misgivings about the talk she was about to give. Maybe it wasn't too late. She could switch to the one the rabbi had approved. Then she saw her mother in the corner of the lobby, aloof and alone. On her own daughter's day she was all but ignored. Penelope had to honor her, make her proud.

She sat in the front row between her parents while the rabbi said a few words about the solemnity of the occasion. She was too nervous to listen. Then he called her up, and in the silence the room seemed to be alive with the movement of ions. She took shallow breaths, her legs like water, but somehow she reached the podium.

"Good morning."

The mic squealed feedback. She stepped away, startled by the sound of her own voice, amplified.

"For my talk this morning, I would like to address the question, what does it mean to be a good Jew?"

Some movement: Yael and his brothers kicking each other in the third row.

"And in these troubled times, does being a good Jew mean the unquestioning support of Israel?" She waited for discomfort: nothing. She continued. "Today, as we watch on television as Palestinian children throw rocks at Israeli tanks, we must remember how the state of Israel began."

Penelope caught sight of her Aunt Celia nodding appreciatively, the gold light from the window catching her earring. The temple smelled deeply of Obsession.

"On April 9, 1948," Penelope recited, "two militia groups, Irgun and the Stern Gang, attacked the peaceful Arab town of Deir Yassin."

A sharp motion to her left: Uncle Saul lurched forward. Cousin Yael had a weird smile pasted on his face.

"By all accounts over two hundred and fifty people were murdered. The militia men sealed families in their homes before razing them. They beat children to death and threw the bodies into wells." People in the audience turned to each other, shaking their heads. Yael kept grinning, wider and wider.

Penelope's heart beat faster. "Women and girls were raped and killed." The words echoed.

"Shame on you!" That was Cousin Zach, rocking his scooter back and forth in the outside aisle. Penelope fixed on Yael's smiling face. A shadow fell on her script; Rabbi Pearlstein had left his seat to stand next to her.

"Today as I become a woman we remember the girls of Deir Yassin who never reached womanhood."

"All right, dear," the rabbi murmured.

She talked rapidly. "And we remember the names of the men who led the assault. Begin! Shamir!" She looked for her mother's face in the crowd and, not seeing it, returned to Cousin Yael's.

"All right, then." He put his hand on her back. "Let's call it a day."

Staring straight at Yael, who grinned wider than ever, she blurted out her last bit before the rabbi could drag her off. "Therefore, in answer to the question, does a good Jew support Israel, we must answer perhaps, but not a good human being."

"Okay, okay," the rabbi said. He stood there while Penelope took her seat on stage.

Penelope's great uncle Mordy, waking from a long nap, called "Mazel tov." His voice cracked the silence.

"We must remember," Rabbi Pearlstein said, "at times like these, the passion and idealism of youth. The young may have much to learn, but if this passion can be harnessed, it can be used to the good of the Jewish people."

Penelope sat on the stage and winked at Cousin Yael.

Only about half the guests stayed for the reception, and Mother greeted them all graciously. Some of the gold-wrapped presents, Penelope noticed, had disappeared. It was a small price to pay. She had spoken truth to power.

During the car ride home only one thing was said, about the time they crossed the Brooklyn-Queens border. Her father said, "At least the food was good."

Penelope sighed. She was looking forward to being alone with her mother.

Later when she was in her room, hashing over the triumph of the day, her mother knocked on the door and slipped in. Penelope, sitting on the bed, hugged her knees in giddy anticipation. Her mother was in a bathrobe, her makeup washed from her face and her hair held back in a ponytail.

"Hi," Penelope said shyly.

Mother closed the door behind her. "How could you do this to me?"

"What?"

Mother grabbed the sash of her robe and yanked it like a noose. The skin on her knuckles was translucent. "Do you want to kill me? There are easier ways to do it, you know."

Penelope turned her head. She could feel the vertebrae grinding in her neck. "I thought you'd like it."

"Like it? We're officially banished from this family now. You understand that?"

"Oh, I don't know."

"Officially banished."

She shrugged. In a day or two her mother would come around. "Maybe that's a good thing."

"Banished."

The client's office was in a row house on a shabby street in Crown Heights. He was just a broker, a middleman: he took in jobs from customers and meted them out to printers, but he didn't do any real printing himself. Penelope reminded herself that each client had to feel like the most important name on their roster. She mounted the front steps and pushed open the door. The corridor was dark, with dingy white and black tile in a faux Egyptian pattern, some of the ceramic chipped, and the building had a mix of smells: sauerkraut, fried onions, metal, cat piss. It felt very comfortable to her. She saw an open door on the right and peeked in. It was a mess of a room, jammed with file cabinets, a wood desk, an old chair on casters, piles of job jackets and cutoffs haphazardly tilting toward each other or away, and a cat or two on top of the piles. A Gateway computer that must have been ten years old sat dead on the floor. A few color wheels from ink manufacturers hung on a wall, and a single, high window let in a beam of yellow light on sparkly particles of dust. Penelope called a couple of times, and finally she heard the flush of a toilet, and a door at the opposite side, which she hadn't noticed, unlatched. The broker emerged, wiping his hands with a paper towel.

He was enormously fat. His pants had a front panel like a sailor's that accentuated his belly, and he wore a synthetic-blend shirt that gaped between the buttons, revealing patches of his undershirt.

And although she knew he was her age, he looked as if he were from a different generation. On his head sat a purple yarmulke embroidered with gold. When he saw her, his tongue moved, and a lozenge clicked against his teeth.

"Can I help you?"

"I'm the senior customer-service agent from Blackwell O'Donnell," she said. "I've come to discuss your job."

"The job was due this afternoon. I assume if you're here to discuss it you missed the deadline."

"It is late," she admitted. "But I thought we could offer you some favorable terms."

He balled up the paper towel and threw it toward an overflowing wastepaper bin. "Could you wait one moment, please?"

"Of course."

"I want to hear these terms of yours. But wait one moment, please."

"Certainly."

He didn't offer her a seat, so Penelope stood in the corner of the office, trying to take up as little room as possible. He steered himself past her, into the hallway, and called down the corridor. "Joel! Asher! Ben! Come here, please."

He walked back into the office, and in an instant three pale young men crowded in the door. Penelope flattened herself against a file cabinet, and the broker lowered himself into the chair.

"All here?" he said. "Very good. You see this woman. This woman has come all the way from Manhattan to tell me that the job her firm has promised to do will miss its deadline. Did she pick up the phone to call? No. Send an email? No. She came herself, the senior customer-service agent, with her heart in her hands, in order to negotiate new terms. This is a woman who values her customers. This is an honest woman. Listen! And learn." He turned to Penelope. "Go ahead, please."

With the young men looking at her, their mouths slightly open, she explained that a longtime client came in with an emergency, and out of loyalty she had to give his job priority. But, because the broker's job was late, she would give him a fifty percent discount, and if his customer would be willing to have his job on forty-pound offset, they could use the leftover rolls from the previous job and incur no cost for paper.

The broker clicked his lozenge. "No paper cost?"

"None. We should have plenty left."

"That's very reasonable." The young men lingered in the doorway, like shirts on hangers. "I'll have to discuss this with my customer, of course. But I will pass on that I think these are excellent terms."

"We do value your business," Penelope said.

"Yes. I'm very impressed."

After a silence, Penelope said, "Don't you remember me, Yael?"

"Should I?"

"I'm your cousin. Penelope."

Yael stood, swaying slightly. "You boys can go." The young men scampered down the hall. Yael took a folding chair that had been resting against the wall and set it up for her. He pulled a handkerchief from his pocket and dusted the seat. "Please. Please. Sit down."

Penelope sat. The office was so tiny their knees almost touched, and she had to twist uncomfortably to avoid grazing him.

"I was sorry to hear about your mother," he said.

"Thank you." Then, remembering her manners, she asked, "How's *your* mother?"

"Oh. Good. You know. My brother Ethan is a physician. Daniel runs a garment factory in Montreal."

Penelope tried to attach faces to these names. She could barely remember them.

"I never saw you after my bat mitzvah," she said.

Yael sucked on his lozenge and nodded. "That was some day."

"I always wanted to thank you."

"Thank me?"

"I remember how you smiled at me. It was encouraging."

"Did I? Probably it seemed funny to me. In those days everything did."

"Still, you seemed very kind. Over the years it's cheered me up to think about it."

Yael's chair squeaked as he leaned back. "I'm sure I didn't mean it that way."

"I think I pissed off a lot of people."

"Nobody blamed you."

"But it was my doing."

"Nobody blamed you. It was the mother."

Penelope took a moment to understand: he meant *her* mother. The use of the third person seemed rehearsed. Maybe he had told others the story of her bat mitzvah. Maybe several times.

"It wasn't, though. She had nothing to do with it."

"No." He waved his hand dismissively. "It was her."

She realized what the bat mitzvah looked like to Yael: a youthful folly. In fact, it shifted everything. It wasn't so long after that her mother started lighting the Sabbath candles, waving her hands over the flames as if she were summoning courage. Then she had a rabbi—not Rabbi Pearlstein, but a rabbi who smelled like fish—come and torch the oven to exorcise nonkosher demons. At first Penelope's father accepted his wife's sudden zealotry with a shrug, but after a couple of years he left her. That didn't stop Mother's march toward Orthodoxy. She charged on with blinkered determination. When Penelope was about sixteen, Mother announced she would take a *mikvah*.

"A mikvah?" Penelope asked. "Isn't that about washing away the shame of menstruation?"

"You're so linear," her mother replied.

On the morning of Penelope's SAT, Mother waded into the sacred water. After darkening an oval Penelope dropped her number two pencil on her desk and said aloud, "Oh, Mother." She imagined her at that moment, Mother's body thin from self-denial, her breasts falling, nipples dark, her pubic hair rusty and wild, stepping into the pool and letting the water lap her—this woman who, as a tough-talking nineteen-year-old, organized the first feminist printing collective in New York—rinsing the sin from her womb, erasing the ligature left by Penelope's umbilical cord.

"Your mother didn't live to see the attacks, did she?" Yael asked.

"No. She had her heart failure the January before." It was actually the elections that did her in. Her mother grew obsessed with chads and absentee ballots. "Everyone's worried about Florida," she told Penelope. "But it's Ohio. Ohio's what you gotta watch." Penelope was encouraged by this brief flare of interest in secular life, as if it might signal a return. But eventually Mother just lost strength and gave up.

"Maybe it's a blessing," Yael said.

"I don't know. She was only fifty-three."

"The things we live to see."

Penelope changed the topic. "Are you married, Yael?"

He shrugged. "Of course."

"Children?"

"Three boys. Just like my father. You?"

"I'm engaged."

"Don't waste time. Married life is a joy."

Men always told her that. She wondered if married life was such a joy for Yael's wife. "How long have you been Orthodox?" she asked.

"Since I met my wife, actually. It's a good way to raise children. You give your day some structure."

Penelope nodded. She wasn't sure if there was anything left to say.

"Why don't we have some tea?" Yael said.

He picked up an electric kettle that had been perched haphazardly over some Pantone books, went to the bathroom and filled it with water, set it back on the books, and plugged it into a surge protector. From a filing cabinet drawer he pulled out a sleeve of Styrofoam cups and a box of Tetley tea bags.

"My mother became Orthodox, you know," Penelope said. "Late in life."

"It didn't matter." Yael placed two cups on top of a job ticket and draped a tea bag in each. His words stung her. "It didn't change a thing."

"I think I drove her to it."

He smiled a little. When the kettle snapped off, the overhead light blazed a little brighter.

"And my mother," he said, "isn't too happy with my direction. She thinks I'm moving backwards. This is what we crawled *out* of, she says." He poured the boiling water into the cups. "Sugar or cream?"

"Do you have any Equal?"

He held the kettle high, looking exasperated.

"Okay. Sugar," Penelope said.

"Crawled out of, like a cave." He got a couple of sugar packets from the filing cabinet and flapped them. After he sweetened her tea, he handed her the cup. "Like you, I wasn't raised this way," Yael said. "My parents wanted to fit in. But as soon as I met my wife, I felt like I was home."

"*Saudade.*"

"Excuse me?"

"It's Portuguese," Penelope said. "Something I heard on the radio. People of the diaspora say it. It's a nostalgia for a place you've never been."

Yael's breathing was labored. She could tell he was moving around more than he was used to. "Not that I don't want to fit in," he continued. "It's just fitting into a smaller space."

"I think I understand."

He settled into his chair and placed his cup of tea on a stained job jacket. "That seems to be the way with our generation." He brought his hands together and divided them, as if he were doing the breaststroke. "Either you become Orthodox or you leave the life completely. My brother goes to a Unitarian church. He says Unitarians don't believe in God, so it doesn't count. I say, 'If they don't believe in God, what's the point of their church?'" He rested his chubby hand on the job jacket. "It's his wife's doing, of course."

Penelope noticed that in Yael's moral universe trouble seemed to begin and end with women.

"But look at you," he said. "Big-time businesswoman."

"I just dress the part."

"You're good at what you do. I can tell. I work with printers all the time. You're good, all right."

"And you. Three pale lads down the hall." She tilted her head toward the adjacent room. "You have your own apprentices."

"My wife's nephews. What choice do I have? They couldn't get a job bagging groceries at D'Agostino."

"Still."

"I'm running a nursery school for adults. About this time in the afternoon I feel like I'm supposed to serve them Hawaiian Punch and graham crackers."

Penelope smiled blandly. "So you're funny. It must be genetic."

"You kidding? Our family wouldn't know a joke if it ran over them with a Zamboni. They're too busy gossiping."

"About what?" she asked, half-dreading the answer.

"Don't get me started. There's more scandal in this family than—you remember Zach?"

"The guy in the wheelchair."

"He's dead."

"Oh."

"Not how you think. He died of food poisoning. Turns out he was on one of those sex tours of Thailand."

"Come on! He was in a wheelchair."

"They make accommodations. The Disabilities Act has opened up all sorts of activities for the handicapped. The differently abled. And Uncle Mordy, you know about him."

"What?"

"Married to Estelle forty years. Turns out he had three kids with the maid."

"No."

"Why would I lie? They live around here, his kids." He gestured toward the street. "I see them in the neighborhood from time to time. If you can imagine three black kids with Mordy's nose."

"Get out."

"I wanted to hire them instead of my idiot nephews," Yael said. "They seem like nice-enough kids. What can you do? I have to keep her happy."

Penelope nibbled on her Styrofoam cup. "You're a nice man, Yael."

"Not really. And all of that's nothing compared to my mother. After my father dies, she pulls out a photo album. My mother in a beehive hairdo and a tight sweater standing next to some grease-ball, leaning on a 1963 Tempest. 'That's Eddie Falnieri,' she tells me. 'He died in Vietnam.'" Yael paused for effect. "'And he's your father.'"

Penelope gasped. "Is it true?"

Yael rolls his eyes toward the ceiling. "Does it matter?"

"Yael! Don't you want to know who your father is?"

"I know who my father is. Bernard Himmelfarb. Unless I stand to inherit that Tempest, I don't see any reason to say anything else."

"You must be curious."

"I would look swell in that Tempest."

Without asking he poured more hot water in her cup.

"They lie, you know," he said. "Our parents. They lied all the time. It always threw me off balance."

Penelope watched the caramel light pour through the window. It was cozy: the light, the lively dust, the stacks of papers leaning like decaying monuments. The three dim-witted nephews. She said, "My mother always told me her favorite part of *To Kill a Mockingbird* was when they say 'Stand up, Scout.'"

"I never saw *To Kill a Mockingbird*," Yael said.

"No?"

"Or read the book."

"Well, there's this scene where all the poor black folk are up in the balcony of the courthouse, and the little girl, Scout, is hiding up there with them, watching her father defend a man who's about to get lynched. When he walks out of the courtroom, they all stand in his honor."

"So?"

"That's *not* what they say. I got the DVD a few years ago and watched it three times just to make sure. The old man says, 'Mary Louise, Mary Louise. Stand up. Your father's passing.'"

"Well. I heard Bogart never said, 'Play it again, Sam.'"

"She lied to me, though. My mother."

"That's not a lie. That's just forgetting."

"But it's completely different. It changes the whole meaning of the line. That old man was too obsequious to have called her Scout. Besides," she said, "it's not cool, all those Uncle Toms bowing and scraping in the balcony. They should have taken Atticus Finch out back of the courthouse and beaten him up for losing their case."

"Now, now."

"Really."

"Keep going and you'll start spouting off about Deir Yassin."

She slapped her hand over her mouth. "I'm done."

He looked at her sternly, from underneath his bushy eyebrows. Then he winked.

"As lies go," he said, "it could be a lot worse."

"I suppose."

"You could have had a wop father."

"Yael!"

He turned away, his big shoulders blocking out half the room. Penelope wondered if he found her worthy of conversion, if he'd invite her to his home to meet his kosher wife and three boys, to light the candles with them as the Sabbath evening fell. Shtetl life—people helping their relatives, living busy and purposeful lives. Everyone in his place. She wouldn't mind spending more of her days wedged into Yael's little office, watching him pour tea and listening to his stories about the blood they shared. If he asked her, she would say yes.

Yael cleared his throat.

"It's getting late," she said preemptively.

Yael hoisted himself from his chair. "I'll see you out."

The wind was beginning to kick up as the sun dropped. It smelled like fall. Yael lowered himself down the stone stairs one step at a time, wincing slightly, as if he had a bad hip.

"I'll get in touch with my customer right away," he said. "Explain the terms. Like I said earlier, they're very good terms, so I don't expect a problem."

She wanted to kiss him, but realized it would be improper, out here in his community. That much she understood.

"Just let us know," she said.

"I'll call—what his name? Ernie?"

"Ernie, yes. He'll be looking forward to hearing from you."

She waited for him to extend an invitation, to determine a next time for them to talk. But no invitation came. And she understood she wouldn't see him again. Not socially. He had no reason to include her in his life. And not in business; he was too humble a client for her to oversee personally.

"Good-bye, Yael." She offered her hand.

He looked at it. "I'm sorry."

She looked at it too, thrust pointlessly between them. "Oh."

"I can't. I'm sorry."

"I know." Men don't touch women in this universe, she remembered. Even cousins. There's too much stench of disgrace. Still she found herself unable to drop her hand, and Yael regarded it as if she'd bared her tit.

"I'll be in touch with Ernie."

He lumbered back up the stairs. Penelope looked up and down the street for a cab, and she started to walk. The wind created little cyclones of trash at her feet—coffee cups, newspapers, Chinese take-out menus—and pieces of paper wrapped around her shins. As she walked, more of it collected on her. Auto-glass circulars, slam-poetry fliers, parking tickets, pages from the *Daily News*, *People en Español*, and the *Forward* clung to her thighs and arms and chest and forehead so she had to walk deliberately, as if she were wearing a coat of mail.

THE GOOD WORD

Inasmuch as Aaron Silver will be remembered, it will be for the Lucky Strike campaign he spearheaded back in 1959. Lucky's sales went flat; Parliament and Winston were hawking their scientific charcoal-recessed filters. Silver, one of the young lions of Madison Avenue, came up with the idea of marketing the unfiltered Luckys to an upscale smoker, one who was tough and took risks—a maverick.

"Lucky . . . uncompromising."

It was only one word, but it shook the industry. Silver was fond of pointing out that it was the sound of the word that reversed Lucky's fortunes, the thumping oompah exhaled through the lips (this was when *The Music Man* was on Broadway; everyone clamored to invoke the rumpus of seventy-six trombones).

Silver parlayed his success into a book on usage cheerily titled *What's the Good Word?* It was meant to be a handbook for other admen, but it soon found its way into high schools across the country, and, through nine reissues, kept Silver's family comfortable even after it went out of print sometime in the late '70s. The photo on the back flap showing Silver in his early, optimistic forties—in a crisp white shirt, tie slightly askew, hands clasped at the back of his neatly barbered head—will no doubt accompany his obituary. Silver has filled out in the cheeks and jowls since his author photo was snapped; some freckles have evolved into fuzzy-edged sunspots. His hair, completely white but unthinned by age, flops to one side like a collapsed chef's cloche.

He watches his daughter—the one that he likes—prepare a pastrami sandwich, cut on the diagonal, as he prefers, with a dill pickle spear and a scoop of coleslaw on the side. He turns to the window. His condo overlooks a children's park, where the wading pool has been drained and lined with interlocking rubber tiles like puzzle pieces. The sun sets. Oak trees drop leaves like stiff and brittle canoes, and the nannies collect the children for the long walk home.

His daughter places the sandwich on his plastic placemat.

"You forgot the skiff," he says.

She breaks into laughter. "The what?"

"You know. The—" He forms a claw with his hand.

"A drink?" she says, still laughing.

Silver grimaces. "That's been happening to me lately. I can't seem to come up with the right card."

The laughter stops. "It's been happening a lot?"

He waves her away. "I'm an old man."

"Maybe you should have Dr. Charleton check it out."

"Dr. Charlatan. What does he know?"

"It might be something he can treat."

Silver watches a camel-colored woman in a sturdy uniform wrap her arm around a boy's waist and carry him sideways, like a log.

"I think my brain is trying to blurt out all the words I haven't used," Silver says.

The daughter he likes sits opposite him and rests her chin on her hand. "That's an interesting theory."

"There's a lot of them. I was watching something on the Discovery Channel the other day. I jotted down some of the vocabulary I haven't had the chance to say. *Fusillade*. What kind of life have I led that I've never had the chance to say *fusillade*?"

"It's not very common."

"But I was *in* the army," Silver says. "*Crankshaft*. That's a good word."

The following day the daughter he doesn't care for shows up, and Silver suspects her uncle, her brother—her *sister*—has asked her to check up on him.

"Come on. I'll take you for a walk," she says.

"What am I? A schnauzer?"

They totter around the children's park. The leaves crunch beneath them. "Look," she says. "They took the water out of the wading pool."

"It's for insurance costs," Silver says. "Some kid drowns in Topeka, and they ban wading pools in New York."

"I guess it's safer."

"Kids get too soft."

She holds his elbow as they walk.

"How's your calliope?" he asks.

"My what?"

"You know. I forget the name."

"Lloyd. He left me, Daddy. I told you."

"It's just as well. He can do better."

The daughter he doesn't care for laughs, a short bark like a mitten's, a *seal's*. She rubs her nose and says, "Someday soon, Daddy, you won't be able to hurt me anymore."

"Betcha can't wait, can you?" His small steps slow to a halt, and he points to the hard ground. "Give me that, will you?"

"What?" She stares where he stares.

He gestures impatiently. "*That*. The parasol, the parapet, the parakeet."

She glances at him, her forehead buckled with worry.

"Look!" he says angrily.

She bends over and pats the ground.

"That. I want that," he says.

"The acorn?"

"That's it. Acorn. Right."

She drops it in his pocket. "Why?" she asks.

"You wouldn't understand." How could she? The first time he saw an acorn, he was nearly grown; it smelled of a life forbidden to him.

She takes his arm, and they continue to walk. "Do you remember when I played in this park?"

"No," he says. "I have no memory of you as a child." This is true. One minute his wife, Bobbie, mentioned she was pregnant. The next he was looking in the rearview mirror at an ungainly young woman wearing an oversized Brandeis sweatshirt and sitting on a footlocker. When she started teaching in the New York City public school system, he pressed upon her a copy of *What's the Good Word?*

She dangled it from her fingers like a dead cod. "We don't teach usage anymore, Daddy. Not like that. Not out of context."

"Why not?"

"These kids grow up with their own usage. It's arrogant to impose an ethnically privileged set of rules. We have to meet them where they're at."

He graciously ignored the preposition with which she ended her sentence. "That's not going to help those kids," he said. "The only thing that separates them from the jungle is correct English."

"That's incredibly racist," she said.

"Don't tell me about racism," he said. He was a longtime member of the NAACP. "And stop saying *incredibly*. You need to retire that word."

Her face bloated, and her eyes filled with tears. He wished she weren't such fun to upset. After she left him, he would brood for a few hours and wind up at the inevitable conclusion: she was too tender, easy to crush as a bird's skull. And if she kept coming around for more abuse, that was her fault, not his. She needed to toughen up. Besides, she had no sense of humor, and how do you talk to a woman with no sense of humor? When, preparing the seventh edition of the book, he updated the text with a chapter on youth-speak and titled it, in her honor, "Like . . . You Know," she flew into a rage. No sense of humor at all.

A week after the walk in the park Silver is in the hospital. The daughter he likes sits beside him, reading the *Times* aloud. Her plate is shining.

"Read the triptych, the trireme."

"What?"

With the IV needles stuck in his arms, he reaches for the paper and emphatically leafs to the penultimate page. "*Here.*"

"The obituaries."

"Yeah. Who died?"

The plankton he likes folds the paper into straight columns, just as he had taught her to do. "No one very interesting," she says. "A president of a mail-order company. A racehorse owner."

"Racehorse," Silver repeats. He closes his eyes. "They put me in a—a whatchamacallit. A caesura."

"An MRI, Daddy."

She knows. Of course she knows. She's the one who fought for it. He heard her speaking to the doctor when Silver was admitted.

"It's not uncommon for old people to stumble over words," the doctor said.

"Not this guy," she said, crossing her arms. "You need to run an MRI. I've been researching."

"We won't be ordering tests right away. Not until he presents with more serious symptoms."

"He needs an MRI," she said. "He obviously has aphasia."

The doctor's face lengthened like a donkey's. "Don't use words like *aphasia* with me."

An eland stands at the foot of the bed, carrying accordion folders.

"This is the lawyer I was telling you about, Daddy," says the one he likes.

The lawyer sits on the bed. "Mr. Silver? Your daughter has asked that you sign power of attorney to her. Do you know what that means?"

Silver nods mutely. Of course he knew. What did they think, he was a furcula?

"In order to transfer POA, Mr. Silver, we need to establish that you are of right mind. Do you understand?"

He raises his finger in agreement.

"Can you tell me what this woman's name is?"

He looks at the shiny dollar he likes. "Of course I can."

"What is her name, Mr. Silver?"

"What's my name, Daddy?"

"Don't you know what your name is?" he demands.

The windlasses erupt into giggles.

Silver smiled. "I know who you are. You're the mother."

"What is she to *you?*"

"The sister."

It isn't quite right. Silver brushes his hand over his forehead. "Come on. You know what I mean. The kid. You're my kid."

The attorney takes his hand and peers into his eyes. Silver enjoys holding the hand of an intelligent young cummerbund.

He awakens to find both of his junipers beside him. It has been ages since he has seen them together.

"I need some drama," he says, parched.

They laugh. "Some water," says the one he likes. She pours him a drink and holds it to his lips.

"You're funny, Daddy," the one he doesn't care for says. "It's like Mad Libs."

"What's that?"

"You remember. That game we used to play, where you randomly replace all the nouns."

"Oh yes. I remember vaguely. Nouns are all I have trouble with," he says. "The other—what are they?"

"Verbs?"

"Verbs. Verbs I know. *Stomp, plead, bleed, point, draw, invoke, chortle, forget.*"

"Very good," says the one he doesn't care for.

"*Patronize,*" he continues.

Her face snaps shut like a blade.

Soon the doctors disappear. Silver rides in a riprap with the boatswain he likes. As they ride he watches the tops of the trees and tries to guess what borough he's in. The big one, he hopes, only he knows that the big borough doesn't have this many pomegranates.

"Look, Daddy. We're in Brooklyn."

"You've brought me here to die," he says.

There's a cross at the head of the bed. The one he likes says, "My father is Jewish," to the pelicans who run the place, and she pries it from the wall. A shadow of the cross remains. The other one doesn't come for a long time. At night when he is alone he is startled to find that he does indeed remember her as a child, a chubby, graceless child. She presented him one Father's Day with an ashtray she made at school (when kids were still encouraged to make ashtrays), asymmetric and glazed a nauseating shade of puce. What did she expect him to do with that?

"It's the ugliest thing I ever saw," he announced.

He watched her face crumple. He felt sorry for a moment, but his regret passed, only to be revived when Bobbie confronted him before bed. "Why must you speak to her like that?" she asked, snapping back the bedspread.

"What? It's just words."

"You of all people."

He wakes, hoping he dreamed it. He hasn't dreamed it. In fact he told his daughter her ashtray was the ugliest thing he'd ever seen.

"Where's the tamarind?" he asks the one he likes, when she appears.

She lifts the water cup.

"Not *that*," he says. "The other one."

She proffers hand lotion.

"Come on," he snaps. "The *other* one." He points out the window.

"My sister. Your daughter."

"Now you got it."

"She'll be here."

His sister's two hollyhocks stand next to his cot and sing Hebrew prayers. Their voices swoop and soar in sequences reaching higher and higher, slightly sour and dissonant. Silver's palm hurts. Their voices are lovely, almost as lovely as their father's, their *mother's*. His sister Ruth's. Saved up every penny, bringing home bundles of cloth to sew, working the treadle with her feet as Avarim (then) lay on the floor and listened to the whir of the bobbin spinning and the thread advancing and the arm shifting up and down, Ruth's hands moving so fast they blurred. With the money Ruth made, she gave Avarim his first dictionary for his bar mitzvah. It was just a kid's dictionary—even at thirteen he knew better—but it was his, with thumb tabs carved into the face and a splatter of blue ink along the page edges. Thorndike and Barnhart. Silver ran his fingers down each column, committing to memory one page per day.

Now Ruth is gone. Bobbie is gone. Silver is alone. Ruth's hollyhocks have grown-up jonquils of their own.

"How are you feeling, Uncle Aaron?" they ask when they are done singing.

"Well, you know," he says. He points to the scaffolding on his head where they drilled. "I have a—whatchamacallit."

"A mass," they suggest.

"A tumor." The one he likes corrects them.

"That's right." Silver points at her. He has taught them: never mince words. Never water them down. Always say what you mean. "A tumor."

The hollyhocks cry and bring their faces close to his. "Good night, Uncle Aaron."

"Good night, Uncle Aaron. We'll see you tomorrow, okay?"

Silver nods. "Yes, yes. Tomorrow."

They leave and he wants to call after them but their gaskets won't come to mind.

He opens his eyes to find the face of the one he doesn't like so much, and his fingers gather the blanket in folds. He has something to tell her but can't recall what it is.

"Very small," he says at last.

He knows what he means to say. Her face shouldn't pucker like that.

"You never quit, do you, Daddy?"

She puts her ungentle hand on his.

"Good-bye, Daddy."

Summoning all his strength, he hoists himself up on his elbows and speaks his last complete sentence. "You mean good night."

She watches his fingers. "Sure. Okay. Whatever."

Silver awakens seized by terror. Too many unused words and many of them—*hypothalamus, heliotrope, ganglia*—unusable. He has a lot left to say. He was eight before Ruth could scrape up money enough to take him to the movies, and as they sat in the balcony, eating jujubes and nonpareils, he watched Charlie Chaplin looking up women's skirts and poking rich people in the butt, and he hoped it would never end. Then the blackness grew, and the picture contracted in an ever-shrinking circle until it was just a dot on the screen, and then it was gone.

He jangles his plastic bracelet against the rail of his cot. The daughter he cares for reads at his bedside, her face a half-moon under the lamp. She looks up.

"What is it?" she whispers, smoothing his forehead.

"Aperture," Silver cries.

UNDERWATER

When Nan moved to Los Angeles, her friends from home sent emails asking if she had seen Jake Gyllenhaal. They asked about other actors, too: Jon Hamm, the guy from *Twilight*, and a couple of Ryans and Joshes that Nan could not keep straight. Her friends imagined there was a critical mass of glamour in Los Angeles that made such encounters likely. Nan's work took her across freeways and into cul-de-sacs, along avenues of nail salons and unfranchised fast-food joints and auto-parts shops and apartment complexes in poor repair with aspirational names like the Patrician or Manderlay Arms. As she lurched along in her Corolla, fish in the backseat, swimming circles in their cellophane bags, she looked at the cars to her left and right. To the left: a very fat woman in a Cutlass eating a Quiznos sandwich out of the wrapper. To the right: a gaunt man in a panel truck with a beard twisted into a long thin braid—he was talking on his cell phone.

The day's first stop was in Hawthorne, a neighborhood close enough to the ocean for an occasional seagull to appear among the pigeons, pecking at french fries flattened on the road, but too far for the beach smells of salt and coconut lotion. Nan pulled into the little parking lot. She set up her salesman's trolley, snapping the bungee cords against freeze-dried packets of cockle, a box of dolomite chips, her tools and test kit, and finally the fish themselves, perched on top of the stack like duchesses, flitting to the north and west to survey their new surroundings: a gray slab of asphalt under a gray sky, the refinery towers of El Segundo not far, emitting whitish smoke. The clinic managers designed the parking lot to provide a buffer of private property against pamphleteers, gunmen, and dough-fingered fanatics who Photoshopped posters of mangled babies. But the fact was the protesters stayed away from this clinic. Jeunessa said they couldn't be bothered with Hawthorne.

Jeunessa was a volunteer who kept the patient roster in order, straightened the magazines, and scolded the doctors for running behind schedule, and it was she who ushered in Nan for the weekly routine maintenance and who kept an eye on her as Nan cleaned the fish tank. Jeunessa was nineteen; the receptionist told Nan she came for an abortion one week and never left. Two or three times they tried to put her on the payroll but something fell through—Jeunessa forgot to produce her Social Security card or complete her security-clearance application. Nan was a tiny bit afraid of her at first: Jeunessa had a claw-peen face, small eyes, a sharp chin, and a paramecium-shaped scar on her left eyebrow. She watched Nan negotiate the front double doors with the cartful of fish gear and did not offer help.

"About time you got here," Jeunessa said.

"It's eight in the morning," Nan said.

"And we open at six."

"You expect me to be here at six? I come all the way from Silver Lake."

Jeunessa stared, her pupils wide and shiny, then her face split into a grin like a sheared rock. "I'm just messing with you."

The thirty-gallon aquarium sat on a table against the wall. Nan rested her trolley beneath it and observed the billowing of anemone. A fish-cleaning shrimp scuttled along the floor, and a foxface rabbitfish flitted toward them.

"That's my friend, right there," Jeunessa said. She tapped her fingernail against the side of the tank. Nan siphoned some water to test for specific gravity and pH and entered the numbers in her log. She scraped the scum from the glass and skimmed the protein from the surface. Jeunessa stood so close her breath warmed Nan's shoulder.

"You bring us something new?"

"Since when are you so interested?"

"You know I don't overfeed those fishies. Just like you told me."

Of all Nan's customers, Jeunessa was the most conscientious—
she and a couple of Armenian auto mechanics in Glendale. Interesting, who kept fish: abortionists, mechanics, dentists, and Chinese
restaurants. Anyone in the business of keeping people waiting.
Nan's chief competitor was an Iranian Jew who was going around
town peddling DVDs of Cirque du Soleil. The Iranian claimed that
the contortionists with their colorful scarves had a calming effect,
tumbling up and down silken strings like marionettes to a Vivaldi
soundtrack that was not exactly in sync, but not disturbingly off-
beat either. He followed Nan's circuit, and she had lost a couple of
accounts to him. One of her clients, a dialysis operator in Gardena,
bought one of his DVDs and showed it to Nan. "No maintenance
costs," he said, by way of apology. "No dead bodies." The day she
collected her tank she fell into a trance watching the circus perform-
ers on the flat screen; they made her feel dizzy and ripped out of
context, the way a couple of hours at a hair salon made her feel, or
attending the family dinner of a distant friend. She did not see how
an endless loop of Cirque du Soleil could possibly soothe anxious
clients. Fish at least had a sense of humor; Cirque du Soleil did not.

"How you get into this business?" Jeunessa asked her.

"The fish game?" Nan surprised herself with her 1950s lingo.
She felt as if she were talking out of the side of her mouth. "I don't
know. I always loved fish. Ever since I was a kid. I think it was grow-
ing up in Colorado, such a long way from any coastline."

"It's a good job," Jeunessa said.

"Tell my parents."

"They don't like it?"

Nan raised her hands in parody. "Four years of college to become
a fishmonger?" She did not come to L.A. to manage fish. She came
to lend money. She had a business degree. She rolled her sleeve to
her elbow, stuck her hand in the tank, and vacuumed the live rock.
After that she slid the tray out from under the tank and, balancing
it on her hip, sidled into the little bathroom where Dixie cups were
always stacked on the toilet tank. The bathroom smelled of milk.

When the tank was reassembled, Nan lowered a bag with a
floating rim into the water. Inside it was an electric blue emperor.
She and Jeunessa watched as he poked the plastic, locomoting his

bag around the tank, suspended just beneath the surface. Jeunessa pressed her nose against the pane. "Blue," she said.

"I thought you might like it."

"'S all right."

"You ever seen Jake Gyllenhaal?" Nan asked.

"Who?"

"My friends from Colorado are always pestering me about spotting Jake Gyllenhaal."

"Not around here." Jeunessa flicked her tongue against the glass. "I did once see this man was on Judge Judy at the Wok Steady."

"Did you talk to him?"

"They don't want you up in their business."

"I suppose," Nan said.

"Why you come here with fish if your parents don't like it?"

"I was afraid of becoming an asshole."

"You're not an asshole." Jeunessa swept her finger along Nan's jawbone.

From the clinic she drove to Alhambra. She inched forward with the traffic on the 710 and listened to talk radio. A headache developed behind her eyes. Alhambra was a long string of Chinese businesses, and it was here that Phil Spector killed a woman, allegedly in his "Alhambra mansion." As far as Nan could see, the neighborhood was nothing but identical mini-malls, two-story white structures built in the '80s, each trimmed with red railings like an ocean liner. She could only imagine the murdered woman crumpling against the plate glass of a licensed foot massagist, Spector's madman hair casting a penumbra around her carcass.

When Nan worked at the bank, one of the other loan officers, a woman named Ellie with rabbity lips, shot a video on her cell phone and sent it to everyone in the office. Within minutes it created a stir. Samuel, who had a shaggy mane and always purred as if he had just awoken, came by Nan's cubicle to watch it with her. The video showed an eviction. A fat black woman in a housedress was threatening the county cops with an eggbeater. "What was she planning to do?" Samuel said. "*Whisk* them?"

The video was three minutes and forty-two seconds, and some-one—maybe Ellie herself—put it on YouTube where it got a couple of hundred thousand hits. Samuel advanced the video to the point when the woman's wig toppled off her head. "It never gets old," Samuel said.

She used to make house calls for the bank. She sat in homes in neighborhoods like Inglewood and Downey in bungalows made of pinkie-thin drywall and hollow-core doors, with loquat trees and bougainvillea struggling in the sandy yards, homes built by develop-ers in the 1950s for the oil and aerospace workers and the meatpack-ers at Farmer John's. When she visited, children and grandchildren hung around, geeky and protective, and cups of coffee were served in family china with a sugared shortbread cookie or a slice of Sara Lee pound cake. She never saw Jake Gyllenhaal at any of these places, either.

The Hunan Palace was always getting written up as the best Chinese restaurant in town, and late at night chic young Asian Americans dined on pork brains or beef balls with tendon. In the mornings, when Nan dropped by to work on the fish tank, the place smelled ripe and yeasty, like a wet carpet, and Mrs. Tong sat by the cash register poring over her receipts. Mr. Tong had a face like a walnut. The two of them snapped at each other in Chinese, their voices pained and querulous.

When she stepped in from the bright day, she had to stand in the red darkness of the dining room before she could move. The tank bubbled in the middle of the restaurant, blue flashes of spotted damsel in the aquarium light. Mr. Tong stepped out of the kitchen and glanced at her, unsmiling. She rolled her equipment to the aquarium as he busied himself about the room, polishing silver-ware and straightening place settings. Because it was summer, the Tong children were not in school. Jenny, who was about ten, sat on the bank by the window, reading a book, and Tyler, a roundheaded boy about six, careened between the tables flapping his arms.

The tank was in bad shape: algae had settled on the little toy houses like a dirty blanket. Food floated on the surface, and a couple of dead gobies were lodged under the Red Sea coral. Nan got her net to remove the corpses.

"You kill those fish," Mr. Tong said. He had been watching her. Mrs. Tong had been watching her too. Jenny looked up from her book. Tyler made engine noises and smashed into a serving cart.

"They were fine last I was here," Nan said. Her peripheral vision narrowed, and her voice sounded as if it were coming from far away.

"You sell us sick fish," Mrs. Tong said.

"I told you not to put too much food in the tank. Look." She pointed to the pellets sprinkling the surface, but they did not look. Nan's hands trembled as she tested the water's acidity. She looked at Jenny, and Jenny dropped her face to the pages of her book.

"You take advantage," Mrs. Tong said. "You think we don't know better."

On how many people did Mrs. Tong use this line? Meat vendors, launderers, restaurant-supply retailers, liquor salesmen. And who knows, maybe some of them did take advantage, although it was hard to see Mrs. Tong letting anyone get the best of her.

Nan started to repack her tools and kits. "You don't like it, get Cirque du Soleil and a plasma screen." She had no idea what was making her so bold. The Tongs were clients she could not afford to lose—they had a fifty-gallon tank and a taste for the costliest, showiest tropicals. Still, she wasn't about to toss more innocent fish to their deaths just because the Tongs paid her.

"Cirque du Soleil dulls the appetite," Mr. Tong said, shaking a spoon at her. "We need fish. You finish your work."

Nan saw the little girl glance up from her book.

"Okay," Nan said. "But no new fish until you learn how to take care of them."

"You finish your work," Mrs. Tong said. Over her head hung signed celebrity pictures of restaurant guests. Robert Blake. Tom Sizemore.

"You ever get Jake Gyllenhaal in here?" Nan asked.

Mrs. Tong squinted through her reading glasses. Then she said something in Chinese to Jenny, who answered quietly.

"Not him," Mrs. Tong said. "The other one."

"Maggie?"

"The other Jake," Mrs. Tong said. She looked at Jenny.

"Jake LaMotta," the girl whispered.

Her last house call as a loan officer had been in Torrance. It was a blindingly hot day. Smog settled in the South Bay so that the sky was neither blue nor white but a kind of rheumy color. The refinery flare stacks shimmered but she could not make out the edges of the flames. Mr. Ramirez—he was younger than Nan, even, but the solemnity of the situation demanded that she call him Mr. Ramirez—was in his front yard when she pulled up and parked. The yard next to his was filled with crazy sculptures: a black Mary with exaggerated breasts, a totem pole carved with Disney characters, a bearded gnome wearing an actual lady's hat. The house itself was covered with a swirling mosaic of broken glass. Mr. Ramirez noticed her staring.

"My neighbor, Mr. Posada."

Nan nodded.

"Crazy old rooster."

"It's beautiful," she said.

"Each to his own."

Mr. Ramirez led her into his own house. It was dark inside, but tidy. There was a round kitchen table made of particleboard with a phony maple veneer, and on it were three straight stacks of paper. They sat at the table. Through an archway she saw the kitchen, a cheerful jumble of onions and gadgets and photos of young children. Nan held her briefcase close to her body. When he saw she was too polite to sit without being asked, Mr. Ramirez tilted his head toward one of the kitchen chairs. He filled a teapot at the kitchen sink.

"If you like we can go over the deed again," she said.

"There's nothing to go over." He did not offer her tea. "I need to refinance and you people won't do it."

"I'm not authorized—"

"Nobody's authorized. That's the way it works, right?" He stood under the arch. He was compact, low to the ground like a mean dog. He did not beg, did not trot out his children or his wailing

wife, did not pull photo albums from a shelf and make her endure
picture after picture of *quinceañeras* and softball games and blindfolded youngsters whacking vainly at a swan-shaped piñata. She
respected him for that. "Right now," he said, "you can't even sell
this place. So who wins?" He took a step toward her. "Can you tell
me that?"

She cleared her throat. "I'm just—"

"Just doing your job."

She wanted some water.

"You got a hell of a job."

After Alhambra her next appointment was in Glendale: the Boule-
vard of Cars. Up and down Brand the dealers had erected twenty-
foot-tall man-shaped streamers that slapped and shimmied with
the trill of pumped air. The lots were full of new cars and the street
was empty. The side alleys off Brand, however, were jumping. Here
the flip side of the car industry prospered: garages, glass dealers,
parts stores, detailers of dubious respectability. Aram and Krikor
ran a body shop that was always jammed full of cars, although Nan
had yet to run into a single customer. There were a lot of employees,
though. All of them young men, fresh from Armenia. They glided
in and out of the lot, rearranging the position of the cars with the
drivers' doors slung open and their left feet dragging on the ground,
yelling to each other in their own language. Sometimes Nan would
hear the moan of a hydraulic lift or the crackle of a blowtorch, but
in general very little work went on. The young men were different
every time she came by; the cars were always the same.

Aram was the big boss. In the trailer his was the inner office,
where his body repair diplomas hung on the wall alongside a cal-
endar that featured women in bikinis brandishing spray guns or
straddling welding machines. There were also photos of Aram's
wife and children and grandchildren against the gauzy blue sky of
a photographer's backdrop.

Krikor kept the books and had a desk in what was also the waiting room, where the fish tank sat on an iron stand. Krikor's desk
was littered with trade magazines and rolls of tabulating paper.
They seemed to have a relationship outside of work—brothers-in-

law, Nan guessed. They were both in their midforties, lean, raw-cheeked. Krikor was balding and Aram shaved his head; when he turned his back to her, Nan could see the bony protuberances at the base of his skull like two fallen parentheses.

Her headache was worse by the time she reached the body shop. When she opened the trailer door, Krikor rose from his desk, bobbling a cigarette between his lips. "You bring us new fish today?"

Cigarette ash coated every surface in the trailer, and the air had the bad smell of smoke and stale coffee and cheap air conditioning. Plants on the windowsill died. Still, the fish thrived; Krikor and Aram followed her directions religiously and told her they'd threatened to fire young men who tried to sprinkle food on the water.

Nan rewarded the Armenians' vigilance with a yellow tang and two surgeonfish. Krikor and Aram watched as she lowered three bags into the tank. The rims of the sacs were buoyed by tiny pockets of air that floated like spill booms. Each fish was in his own habitat, darting around the tank in his private balloon. Nan's headache throbbed behind her left eye. She drew water from the tank with a pipette and squirted a few cc's into each of the bags.

She stopped to massage her forehead. "Do you have an aspirin?"

"I got something better than aspirin," Krikor said. He went to his office and came back with a plastic bottle with Cyrillic script. "I get this sent to me."

"Is it ibuprofen?"

"You got a headache?" Aram asked.

"The change in air pressure," Krikor said. "I feel it too. I think we get some rain."

Nan looked at the patch of sky through the high slit vent of the trailer. It was not going to rain; it never rained.

"You got a headache, this takes it away." Krikor snapped his fingers.

"Will I be able to drive?"

He pursed his lips. "Drive? Of course. It's strong, but it's not a narcotic. I get you some water."

While Krikor was in the bathroom, one of the young men stumbled in, wearing an oil-stained Angels cap. Aram snatched the cap off the kid's head and used it to slap his shoulder. They watched as Nan transferred more tank water into the float bags. Aram said something to the young man in Armenian, and then he straightened himself and said, "I tell him what you do. Getting the fish used to the new water."

"Acclimating," Krikor said, cracking the word on his palate. "You have to do it gradually." He put a cup of water and two red tablets on the pane of glass that covered half the tank. Nan looked at the tablets dubiously. The pounding in her skull jabbed in their direction. She swallowed them.

The first time she saw the video of the woman losing her home and her wig, it was in the privacy of her own cubicle, and she didn't know it was supposed to be funny. She was puzzled. Then she heard laughter erupting from one nearby desk, then another, and Samuel draped himself over her divider to watch it with her, and by the fourth or fifth time she was laughing herself. She wasn't faking it, either. As her co-workers watched the video, stopping and rewinding the best parts, inserting their own sound effects and dialogue, she regarded them with something like love, and the hilarity that swelled in her belly and bubbled up her windpipe smudged the edges between them. They were limp with laughter, draped over the desks and the monitor, shoulders and jaws quivering and uvulas waggling in their open mouths—a breathing, tearful organism.

The walls of Krikor's trailer began to bend, and the shelves full of chrome fenders rattled. She went down; Krikor had grabbed her collar and pulled her to the desk in the center of the room, and the four of them crouched—Nan and the three Armenians. She saw the young kid's face damp with fear. Aram said something in Armenian and then in English: "Look at him afraid. It's just an earthquake."

"Welcome to California," Krikor said.

Nan watched the aquarium sway a little on its iron stand. The fish displayed their tails in bright gay splotches. When it was over, Krikor said, "We should go outside. In case of aftershocks."

"How are the fish?" Aram asked. They stayed in their crouch.

"The fish are okay," Krikor said. "The water absorbs the shock."

They sat with their knees to their chins and watched the tang nudge the rim of his bag. Beneath her hands Nan felt the grime on the trailer floor. "My friends always ask me if I've seen Jake Gyllenhaal."

"I haven't seen him," Krikor said. "You seen him, Aram?"

"Who is that?"

"You know. The gay cowboy."

"No," Aram said. "We seen the other one. His father used to be on *Sea Hunt*."

"Bridges," Krikor said.

"Jeff?" Nan asked.

"The brother," Aram said.

"Beau?"

"Beau. We seen him buying spinach at the Whole Foods. You tell your friends we seen a very great man."

SEVEN REASONS

1. Rage

Not the kind of rage that swells and bursts and leaves you ragged. Just the normal, everyday rage that expands and contracts with your pulse, that can be brought on simply by sitting in the dispatcher's office with Pidgen, Stepple, and Moroni and listening to Pidgen tell, for the twenty-third time, about the night he nearly ran out of gas on the I-95 South, and how he had no choice but to exit in a bad section of Wilmington and stop at a Chevron station where everyone, *everyone*—the other motorists, the girl behind the bulletproof Plexiglas, the panhandler stumbling around with a squeegee—was (here Pidgen passes a hand over his face to indicate they were black), and Stepple, whose lazy eye watches you even though he's looking at Pidgen, whistles yet again in appreciation of Pidgen's courage, and Stepple dribbles a wet tobacco leaf on his lip like a parsley garnish, and again recites how he manfully ordered his wife to lock all the doors and seal the windows as he pumped gas, to save herself, if she needed to, and not to worry about him. And one more time Pidgen sighs, "I was lucky to get out alive."

Or the heat you experience when you drive home listening to the sports radio station poll its listeners on the Greatest Sports Moment of All Time, and the winner is not the obvious (Jackie Robinson bunting in the seventh to bring home the winning run in his first game at Ebbets Field) or the second most obvious (Billie

Jean King trouncing Bobby Riggs) or even the third most obvious (Ali. Foreman. Rumble in the Jungle) but the U.S. Olympic hockey team beating the Russians in 1980. Any world that crowns a hockey game as the Greatest Sports Moment of All Time is a world that's too depressing to live in.

Now my co-worker Sammy Bonavitacola, wearing his bright yellow slicker fastened with Velcro at the collar and open at the tails and flying behind him like a cape, strolls toward me on the catwalk, clanging a pipe wrench along the railing just to hear it ring. He isn't five years old, by the way. He's thirty-five. His yellow slicker is the only splash of color against the fall day: not quite raining, but not dry, either, and add to that the clouds of steam rising from the cooling towers beyond the railroad tracks, the patches of dead weeds, the rail ties drenched in creosote, the slate-colored tank cars lined up on each side of the walkway, and we're working within a pretty narrow range of grays and blacks.

"Thought you might like some company," he says.

I'm loading a railcar with liquid propane. Pipes, articulated like spider legs and coated with frost, run from the catwalk to the open hatch of the car. The last thing I want is Sammy Bonavitacola's voice jamming up my brainwaves.

"Hey, look," he says, pointing. "Some poor slob is coming down the track."

We watch a figure to the south. But I think Sammy's wrong. It's not a person. It's one of those person-shaped signals along the right-of-way. You've seen them from the coach window: round head, red and green lights like eyes and mouth, crossbar like arms. That's what it looks like anyway. But I know where all the semaphores are, and this one is new, and it seems to be approaching.

2. Opportunity

Hasn't everyone who's worked around railcars faced the temptation? That swift twelve-foot drop from hatch to ground. Of course, the fall is complicated by the curve of the vessel. If you ride down, as you would on a playground slide, you land on your feet with a couple of broken ankles. Head first and your troubles are over, if you're lucky. If you're not, you end up like Christopher Reeve, minus the good looks and the Superman residuals.

But there are other methods. The safety valve, for example. Don't open the vent line, and once the pressure tops four hundred psi, the safety valve will rupture with a force that can shear your head from your neck. And you've got the tank-car wheels, each taller than you are, and the smooth and silvery groove where the rim of the wheel hugs the rail. The cars are braked and chocked, of course. But release the brake, kick the chock out from under the arc of the wheel, and the car will roll. It may look as though it's on flat ground, but it will roll and gather speed like a horse, and it will have the sense to head out the gate and back to the switching yard.

Especially if you are not the type to seek revenge, if you have no one to punish and would just as soon avoid the grand gesture, the Biblical language, the opera. If it's simply a case of not being able to move from one minute to the next, the railroad provides a barrel of choices, any of which can look like a credible accident. Just pick one.

And if there are people who work along the railroad who haven't thought of this, well, they're just not thinking.

Sammy is playing with the gas sniffer, slung around his neck like a tourist's camera, and he shakes the wand this way and that as if he were prospecting for gold.

"Hey, let's see which of us is more toxic," he suggests.

He unsnaps the fly of his coveralls and sticks the wand in his pants, squeezes his eyes shut, inflates his cheeks, and farts. The needle on the dial springs to eight on the scale, bordering the red zone.

"Can you top that?"

I let him stick the wand down my back. It tickles my spine, and when I feel the tip cool against the crack of my ass, I let one rip.

"Sweet fucking Christ," Sammy cries. "Ten on a scale of ten." He pulls the wand out of my coveralls. It feels creepy, like getting an IV pulled out of my veins. "You are way too much woman for me. At least you got a marketable skill to fall back on if you decide to quit loading tank cars." He wipes the wand with an oil rag and aims it south. "It's definitely a dude." He's right: the semaphore has arms and legs. It carries a suitcase.

3. Futility

Check out this newspaper story. Single mom moves out of Wilmington, into the suburbs to raise her boy. Even though she's working on the GM assembly line and has a second job delivering flowers out of a van, she reads to him, attends teacher-parent conferences, helps him with his homework, saves her pennies to send him to Catholic school. Kid plays basketball, gets good grades, wins a full scholarship to Penn. Goes out with some friends to celebrate the scholarship, cops pull over their car and spread the kid against the wall, kid starts mouthing off, cop shoots him in the head.

The point is, there's no point to doing anything. Remember that the next time you go to the gym.

Sammy is babbling about a stripper he had yesterday in a room over Walt's House of Calamari in Claymont, a woman whose talents, according to Sammy, include masticating a banana without having to open her mouth. "A wonderful girl," he says, "and still I couldn't close the deal."

I wait for Sammy to finish his sordid tale and leave. I got something I got to do.

"It's a question of hygiene," he says.

Sammy has a Prince Valiant haircut he's much too old for. I suspect he dyes it. His bangs flatten with sweat beneath the vinyl band of his hard hat. He peers down the track. From the catwalk we can see all the way to Wilmington or to Chester, depending which way you turn.

"That guy's coming this way. Look."

A man in a beige suit, just discernible against the fog.

4. Fear

Not of heights: heights are easy. You couldn't last one day on this job if you had a fear of heights. Same goes for a fear of being alone, of loud noise, of rats. But you should hear the ice cream truck that prowls these streets at night. No one seems to be driving; it skulks on its own between the empty warehouses and maintenance sheds, crawling around the industrial landscape where you wouldn't spot a child within five miles. And that tinny melody coming from its speakers. Not a normal ice cream jingle, like "Pop Goes the Weasel" or "Für Elise." No, this truck broadcasts "Bohemian Rhapsody," as it might sound on a demented harpsichord. God only knows what's festering in the bowels of its freezer compartment. Get off work after double overtime—two, three in the morning—and there it is, turning toward the river, its silver hasps catching the light of the flare stack.

"If I was by myself, I'd think I was hallucinating," Sammy says. The man in the beige suit is close enough that we can see something is not quite right. It's not that he's missing an arm or walking with a limp or that his jacket is buttoned wrong.

"That's the problem with this job," Sammy continues. "Too much time alone. When you're up here loading these cars, six or seven hours can go by and you don't talk to a soul. It's not healthy. Hey, do you do that thing where the cars talk back to you?"

I stare at him.

"You know, like each car's got a personality," he says. "For me they're characters out of black-and-white movies. You know those Southern Pacific cars, the ones with the hatches that are really tough to crack, when you gotta get a four-foot wrench with an extension? I hear them talk like a gangster. *I'm tellin' ya, copper, you'll never take me alive.*" Sammy holds out his wrists and dangles his fingers like Cagney. "Or the white propane cars, the ones that are stiff at first, but once you give them a good yank, the fitting comes off like butter?" He smoothes his hands over his hips and undulates. "*All right, big boy, I guess you—unh—got me where you want me.*"

Mae West.

"Then you got your Conrail cars, the new ones, which always behave when the others are acting up. I hear them as a guy with a little mustache and an English-type accent. *Now see here, gentlemen: what seems to be the trouble?*"

Potential Reason Number Eight: the people you work with appear to be insane.

5. Fatigue

Even if you can remember being a fairly energetic person, someone who jogged around the neighborhood as the storekeepers cranked open their awnings and hosed down the sidewalk, now there are whole hours when you cannot move a finger. Finish loading the tank cars and sit in the toolshed while the gray of the day turns to purple and then black. It's all you can do to walk back to the locker room, peel off your coveralls, and step into the shower. And tomorrow you have to do the same thing. See Reason Number Three.

"It's a hobo." Sammy perches on the lower rung of the handrail to get a better look. "You don't see that too much anymore. When we were kids we used to see them all the time. Railbirds. Sometimes one would come around the backyard, and my mother would make him a sandwich."

The hobo is even with us, on the tracks that Conrail shares with Amtrak—still a good thirty yards away and separated from us by the cyclone fence. He is sure-footed, accustomed to walking railroad tracks. And his suit isn't so much beige as worn down to its batting. It must have been a good suit, once; he even wears a vest. And now that he's close, we can see what makes him look peculiar: he's smiling. Then he does a funny thing. He stops walking, lowers his suitcase, opens it up, and starts fishing around. It's a cheap cardboard suitcase, and his belongings seem to consist of balled-up scraps of newspaper. He pulls something out and holds it in the air to inspect it.

"What's he got there?" Sammy asks.

The hobo moves his hand with a flourish. The object opens and closes.

"Scissors," Sammy says.

As we watch, the hobo reaches behind his head, curving his arms with a dancer's grace, lifts a hank of hair, and snips it. The clump of hair flies toward Wilmington. He snips again. Another chunk of hair is carried away on the breeze. Snip, snip, snip. When he is done, he pats his scalp, feeling for tufts he may have missed.

Sammy takes off his hard hat and pushes his matted bangs from his forehead. "I could use a touch-up myself."

6. Humiliation

The most underrated of emotions. All those Greek plays we had to read in high school, the ones about high crimes and the high sentiments that triggered them, they got it all wrong. Jealousy, desire, grief—they don't compare to humiliation. Those other emotions eventually fade. But think back to your most embarrassing moment. Maybe it happened five years ago, maybe ten. Bet you anything it still has the power to make your heart rush and your face prickle and the back of your neck grow warm, as fresh as if it were yesterday. Maybe you went to the company picnic in a white sundress on what turned out to be the first day of your period, and while you were balancing your paper plate full of egg salad and pickled beets, a stain like a rose bloom spread from your crotch. Maybe you returned the flirtatious wave of a boy you hankered for, only to realize he was looking at the girl standing behind you. Maybe you once pleaded with a man to abandon his wife, your eyes running, your nose running, your voice choked with sobs. And maybe a year later you ran into the same man, after you'd told everyone you know how you would cut out your heart (pound chest for emphasis) to get him back, and you noticed that he used phrases like "if you will," that the lenses of his glasses were smudged with fingerprints, and that he had an odor on him like sour milk.

Humiliation is the king of passions. That's why when people recount their worst anecdotes, they always end up saying, "I felt like dying."

After the hobo cuts his hair, he packs up his scissors and his balls of paper, collecting a few shreds from the ground where they scattered, buckles up his suitcase, and sets it along the rail tie. Then he jiggles it, testing its stability, and sits on top of it facing north toward Chester. He places his hands on his lap and leans into the draft, closing his eyes like a collie hanging its head out the car window.

"I guess he's taking a rest," Sammy says.

We feel the plate rumble beneath us and the valves clatter in their casings. Our bones vibrate. Sammy looks at his watch. "The 2:13 freighter from Philly to Baltimore," he says. "Right on time, too."

7. Regret

Say you're fourteen, and you're making out with Gary Pilecki in your parents' basement. And say Gary Pilecki is seventeen, and already has enough facial hair to grow a real three-day stubble, and you're seeing that stubble closer than you'd ever dreamed of, and it's scratching your face, and his hand grazes your breast, and pinches your nipple, and rests on the zipper of your jeans, and you think he's going to put his fingers inside your pants, when your eight-year-old brother who has been playing upstairs discovers how to shift his transformer from robot to car, and he charges down the steps to show you, carrying his toy in front of him like a torch. Say, then, you jump up and scream, "Jesus, you are such a stupid idiot." And the little brother's face dissolves from pride to a whole blend of things, like surprise, hurt, love. Not anger. If there'd been anger, you could live with it. And you remember this ten years later when the brother signs up for the army, even though military service is as far outside your family's experience as contortionism. And again when he returns, his skin unbroken but what's inside of it different, somehow; and now, when he drifts around North Carolina, operating carnival rides in the summer and poaching Christmas trees in the winter, getting blow jobs in the back rooms of pool halls, phoning you every few months and demanding six thousand dollars so he can go to Oregon and raise alpacas. And you remind yourself that, despite this turd of a life he leads, this is your brother, his body is the body you lifted out of the tub and swaddled with towels, the baby who wriggled his toes and said, "Don't forget my feets!" as you patted him dry.

The worst part is this: even as you gazed at that shiny face, all you could think about was whether you still had a shot at getting Gary Pilecki's fingers inside your pants.

Actually, the worst part is this: given the right circumstances, you still have it in you to say it again.

Sammy says, "I hope he's not on the wrong track. When that freighter comes, it comes fast." He checks his watch again. Sammy's yellow raincoat starts to billow in the headwind of the oncoming train. Then we hear the signal: two long toots followed by a short and a long, standard for an engine approaching a town. A few seconds later the headlight over the cowcatcher glitters to the north. "Here he comes."

The hobo still leans forward. He opens his eyes and slaps his knees three times.

"Come on, champ," Sammy mutters. He wants the hobo to jump off the track. Not me. I respect the tramp's dedication. In fact I haven't felt this alive in months.

The train signals again, only this time it's three long blasts. Someone or something on the track. My teeth chatter.

"Ten bucks he brakes," Sammy says. The engineer is not supposed to brake. Everyone knows that. Even though the instinct kicks in hard and human, it's an instinct he has to override. He can't stop the train in time, and he runs the risk of a derailment: ninety cars packed with liquefied petroleum gas, tumbling off the track like toys. It takes a lot of training and experience and presence of mind, but once a jumper is in his sights, the engineer's best choice is to comply with his wishes.

Beads of moisture from the cooling tower collect on our faces and start to freeze. The engine dwarfs the man on the suitcase. His heroism is dreadful. A lump turns in my stomach as if I have swallowed a cough drop, and the space between the catwalk and the ground opens up beneath me like a trapdoor. I grab Sammy's wrist and yell, "What are we supposed to do?"

"Nothing we can do."

The hobo looks up at the engine and raises his right hand to his forehead in a military salute. Sammy returns the salute with his free hand. "Godspeed, pal."

The hobo teeters back on his suitcase and crumples beneath the wheels. I look at the engineer in his cab. His jaw is open; he must be screaming. But to his credit he doesn't brake. The draft slaps our faces and whips up the hem of Sammy's slicker; the grommet hits my cheekbone.

"Good set of nerves," Sammy says.

As the cars pass by, I release his arm and turn away. "I don't want to see."

The last car recedes in the distance. We're back to the usual noises: pumps running, the tank cars humming as they fill with product.

"Not much to see," Sammy says. "No body parts or nothing. Just a bundle of clothes on the track."

My knees buckle. I grab the railing on the way down and pretend I'm stooping.

"You okay?"

"I dropped something." My legs won't work. I sit on the metal plate of the catwalk.

"You sure you're okay?"

"Just taking a seat."

Sammy disappears into the toolshed. When he reappears, he says, "I called dispatch. They're gonna notify the rail cops."

He sits next to me on the floor. We prop our backs against the handrail and stick our legs out in front of us. The catwalk is so narrow the soles of his Red Wings tap against the kick guard. "Tic Tac?" He pulls a box from his breast pocket and rattles it. Then he pours a few green ones into my hand. They don't have much of a flavor, but put enough of them in your mouth at once and you can detect a trace of mint. It's something, I guess.

GEOGRAPHY

We noticed the stain in late March, me and Taurus and Clark. Thaw: the season of renewal and repair in an oil refinery. Gaskets burst and flanges seep, ice melts off the pipelines and the ground softens, sucking the soles of our boots. Taurus and I stepped around a blotch in the soil too dark to be mud. We plumbed its depth with our box wrenches. Naphtha, the refinery mutt, flattened his paws and lowered his snout. Then Taurus did the same thing—got down on his hands and knees and lowered his nose to the earth.

"What are you doing?"

"I'm recreating Naphtha's actions," he said. "My daughter learned this in theater club. It's called Method acting." His nostrils quivered over the stain. "To smell like a dog, you have to behave like a dog." He nodded, stood up, and brushed off his coveralls. "Crude," he pronounced. "I would say high sulfur, low API, by the smell of it."

I glanced around at the tanks, brilliant and whitewashed in the cold sun, all of them full of gasoline for the springtime rush. "There's no crude around here."

"Oh, but there is," Taurus said. He turned to climb the fire bank, back to the truck. "There's the Secret Crude Line."

"There's no Secret Crude Line." I didn't want to look gullible.

"Not that anyone talks about."

Taurus got a plastic bottle from the truck bed and went back to scoop up some dirt. He had a face like mashed potatoes squished into a pie pan. We were the field operators so we rode together all shift, pulling samples, reading gauges, and spinning the occasional valve. I wished he were handsome, like Clark, our dispatcher, but Taurus was funny, and he listened to the jazz station out of Temple, and he taught me how to drive a stick in the company pickup. He came to work in brightly colored tracksuits and flip-flops and lounged around the break room in his civvies until the foreman made him put on his uniform.

Since the big layoff there were only four of us on the crew: Clark, Taurus, me, and Kreigel, and Kreigel never did any work, so it was like we had three. Technically Kreigel was a field man, too, but he spent all his time with Clark in the control room, doing what he called police work: masquerading as a little girl on the web, trolling for predators. We called the little girl "Heidi," which pissed him off. "Laugh all you want," he warned us. "There's a sickness out there."

We found Clark at his console, the red and green lights of his control panel blinking on the walls around him. Clark had the posture of a Marine, flat and taut, and he walked with a forward pitch like a praying mantis. He spent a few minutes at the start of each shift setting his desk just the way he wanted it: his logbook opened to the current date, a row of pencils sharpened to dagger-points on the right-hand side, his coffee mug on the upper right, and next to it a 50-cc sample bottle filled with Maalox. Clark wore a ball cap with the visor pulled low over his eyes, and he kept the radio tuned to the country Top 40 station.

Taurus slammed the plastic bottle on Clark's desk blotter. "Look what we found by the Casinghead Line."

"Been on your knees, looks like," Clark said.

"I was investigating. Just like Heidi over there."

Kreigel blurrily glanced up from his computer screen. "Go ahead and make fun."

Clark sniffed at the bottle. "Crude."

"That's what I was telling her."

He meant me. "Her" in a work context meant me. In a home context it meant a guy's wife. It took me a few months to realize "I was telling her we need to refinish the basement" meant "I was telling my wife . . ."

"It's a leak the shape of Maine," I said.

"I was thinking more like Rhode Island," Taurus said. Taurus was in love with Rhode Island. "The only state smaller than Delaware," he said triumphantly. He wanted to go there someday and plant a Delaware state flag.

"The Secret Crude Line," Clark said.

"I told you," Taurus said. "Didn't I tell you? She didn't believe there's a Secret Crude Line."

Clark removed his ball cap and put on his hard hat. His coveralls were always spotless, and I swear to God he pressed them. "Hold the fort, Kreigel?"

Kreigel waved at us, his eyes fixed on his monitor.

At the leak we walked around the periphery. Naphtha jogged along the fire bank and waited for us with his mouth hung open.

"Looks like the LP failed," Clark said.

"What's the LP?" I asked.

"The leak preventer."

I looked at his face. I could only see the lower half, and the straight line of his mouth was inscrutable.

"You're kidding me, right?" I looked at Taurus. "There's no such thing as an LP."

"Not if it doesn't prevent leaks," Taurus said.

I could never tell when they were joking. Nothing was called what it was supposed to be, and everyone had a different name. Mine was Little Shit—Little Bit for the older guys who were too proper to curse in front of women. Taurus's real name was Carna-han, but fifteen years earlier he and a barmaid had been cut out of his smashed-up Ford, so we called him Taurus in case a day should go by that he didn't think about it.

Clark's logbook had a fancy binding and pages of graph paper, and Clark entered notable events in his small square print, one let-ter to a box. "Discovered leak in the Secret Crude Line 27 March," he wrote. Then he added, "Roughly the shape of Maine." One point for me.

When Clark told the shift foreman, he replied, "Come on, Clark. You know there's no Secret Crude Line."

The following week we swung to the evening shift. Early eve-ning was Heidi's busiest time, after school and before the predators were busy with their own wives and families, so Kreigel stayed in the pump house and clicked away at his keyboard as we charted the stain's progress. I said it was beginning to look like Illinois.

"It's a good thing you know geography," Taurus said. "We'd have no words for it otherwise."

Clark rubbed his knuckles on his forehead, just under the band of his hard hat. "This thing gets any deeper it'll get in the ground-water." He walked back to the pump house to write in his log, leaving the truck with Taurus and me. Naphtha followed him back, sweeping his tail in long low strokes.

"What have we here?" Taurus crouched to the ground and poked with his finger. He pulled out a flask-shaped bottle, the color of cobalt and the size of a hundred-count aspirin jar, embossed with a bunch of grapes. "Blue glass. Not very common. In my lifetime used only for milk of magnesia and Noxzema, and they both went to plastic decades ago. But this," he said, polishing the bottle on the leg of his covies, "predates either of them. The leak must have stirred it up to the surface."

On the ride back we listened to Ella Fitzgerald, and Taurus enjoyed it so much he drove into town just to go on listening. We went past the pawnshop and the furniture rental, down a residential street lined by frame houses with sad porches, where women lounged with their little girls. When they saw the company truck, some of the women came down from the porches, and when they saw me in the passenger seat, their faces went dead and they backed away. All the women were white, but many of the little girls were black. They didn't have fiercely plaited cornrows like the children in Chester, bedecked with plastic flowers. Instead they had untamed, anvil-shaped naturals, proof of their mothers' helplessness with black hair. One girl even had a comb still lodged in her curls, as if her mother got so frustrated with grooming she just gave up.

We kept driving up a hill to a plateau near the interstate, and Taurus turned the truck around and pointed the grille toward the river so the sun set behind us and we could watch the refinery lights come on all over the tristate area. "Every night is Christmas," he said.

The disc jockey had a sleepy voice, and occasionally our walkie-talkies crackled in their holsters and Clark broke in, asking our twenty and calling us home. The DJ put on some West Coast jazz, and Taurus said, "That really swings." He propped his elbow out the open window and clicked his wedding ring against the frame in a complicated rhythm. "I lived on the West Coast once."

"You did not."

"For a whole year. San Francisco, after I got out of the Navy."

Taurus was full of surprises. "Did you like it?"

"Loved it. When gay men constitute a critical mass of a given population, the odds for heterosexuals skyrocket. Even ugly guys like me have a shot."

"You're not ugly."

We returned with some hoagies to make Clark forget we'd been AWOL, and we found him glaring at the back of Kreigel's head. "He wants to know how to spell *cunnilingus*," Clark said.

"Two *n*'s," Taurus said, unpacking the sandwiches.

"*Cunnilingus* has three *n*'s," Clark corrected.

"Why would Heidi know *that*?" I asked.

"Well, yeah, if you count all the syllables," Taurus said.

Kreigel spun around. "Quit calling her Heidi," he said. He was a big Dutchman, wide in the hips, with a face pocked like a loofah.

"What do you call her?" I asked.

"I go by different screen names," he said. "It keeps them on their toes. This is serious work, and I got the deputy's badge to prove it."

"Hey, I got one of those," Taurus said. "I think it was for giving ten bucks to the Police Boys' Clubs."

"To hell with you, Taurus."

"He's breaking your stones is all," Clark said.

But Taurus was laughing. "Yeah, I think my kid got one of them, too. Genuine plastic."

Kreigel jumped up and started towards Taurus. I hadn't seen him on his feet in a while, and I'd forgotten how big he was. At least six feet and a good two-fifty, most of it settled low like down in an old parka.

"For God's sake, sit down, Kreigel," Clark said. "Go on back to your work. Taurus, sit down and eat your hoagie and leave him the hell alone. You too, Little Shit. Sit on the hell down. Damn, Kreigel, they're just breaking your stones."

But Kreigel put on his hard hat and headed outside, and Taurus was still laughing when we sat down to eat.

Taurus and Clark had the same first name: Scott. It wasn't a problem since no one called either of them Scott. I'd been working with him for six months before it occurred to me Clark even had a first name—he was grand enough for a unimoniker, like Prince. Clark was Clark, and no one dared to coin a nickname for him, even behind his back. We called Kreigel Hole-in-the-Pocket because he jerked himself off during the graveyard shift, when he assumed everyone was asleep. I thought this was an exaggeration until the night I woke up, in the red and green light of the control room, and noticed the fabric of his coveralls rolling over his lap and his head tilting back. I had to pee, but kept my face against the desk a good ten minutes before he finally got up to splash himself at the water fountain.

After we finished our hoagies, Kreigel returned and threw his hard hat on the floor. "I didn't find any blue glass," he grumbled. "I didn't find any goddamn glass at all."

"Where there's one there's more," Taurus said. He had a tiny piece of banana pepper stuck in the corner of his lips. "My guess is we hit an old and ancient trash dump."

Kreigel logged on to his chatroom. "Clark, I went ahead and closed that header by the kero pump."

"We're leaving that open for line washes," Clark said.

"Oh, since when is that, now?" Kreigel asked.

"Since two, three months ago," Clark said. "If you're going to keep your head rammed up your ass, I'll ask you to stay the hell out of my tank farm."

Taurus got a kick out of this. Every evening we described the stain for Clark: Texas, Alaska, Mali. Then we dug for glass. Naphtha came too, pushing aside detritus with his paw as if he were unwrapping birthday presents. The ground was sodden and gave up rose glass, or green, or amber. We spit on the bottles and wiped them and lined them up at the window back at the pump house so they refracted the fading light, and Clark entered the size and shape of the stain in his log.

"Aren't they going to do something about it?" I asked.

"Haven't you heard? The Secret Crude Line doesn't exist."

"So why do you keep entering it in your log?"

"Ever hear of cover your ass?"

We swung onto the graveyard shift. It was too dark to hunt for glass, so after our rounds Taurus and I rode around in the truck, listening to overnight radio and looking in the distillation units for anyone who was awake and available for gossip. By two in the morning most everyone had crawled off to sleep, and Taurus, who never slept, not even at home, returned us to the pump house. We hung out in the break room, which was decorated with some dusty tinsel garlands and strings of jalapeño lights that guys had put up for a Christmas party years before and no one had bothered to dismantle. Taurus was reading a book about Chernobyl, and I dozed off with my head against the wall. When I woke up, Taurus was gone, and Kreigel was rummaging through the refrigerator. I stamped my foot awake, and he grunted.

"How long you three think you can get away with this?" he asked.

"What?"

"Clark and Taurus, they don't see," he said, crouching at the salad crisper. "Contamination. *Moral* contamination. It's crept into the substrate."

I nodded.

"In Japan grown women dressed like schoolgirls are prowling the Ginza. This is the level we're dealing with here." He backed away from the fridge with a yogurt in one hand and a head of cabbage in the other. "Back during the Great Shortage, Frankie Popovic wrote down the name and flag of every loaded tanker in demurrage. They were hanging three deep off the docks, the hell they weren't. Fresh from Nigeria and chock-full of oil. Then the state troopers stopped old Frankie on I-95 and found enough five-gallon gas cans in his trunk to flatten Rehoboth. They can have you disappear, make no mistake. Turpitude."

He marched off with his produce and dairy. The light through the window was predawn and grayish. Somewhere a machine was whirring. I walked down the hallway toward the noise and a green glow and found Clark in the copy room, xeroxing the pages of his log. Sheets of paper flew off the delivery tray. He scooped them up in fistfuls and shook them at me. "Documentation, Little Shit."

When we rotated back to day shift, Clark growled at any boss who happened to come into the pump house. "We need a backhoe," he said. "We need a pipe fitter. We got a sinkhole in the ground like Zimbabwe."

"More like Zaire," Taurus coached from his chair.

Clark shot Taurus a look. "There *is* no Zaire. It's the Republic of Congo."

"We're doing our best, Clark," the boss said. "We have to go through channels."

"It's the Secret Crude Line."

"Oh, come on, Clark," the boss said amiably. "You know there's no Secret Crude Line. That's just an old wives' tale."

Clark pressed his forearms against his desk blotter. "How many old wives you know sit around talking about petroleum products?"

Taurus picked up his hat and motioned for me to follow him outside. Spring had settled in; a few puffy clouds floated like gondolas. We watched a white-rumped doe canter across the tank farm, with Naphtha in pursuit. The doe extended her forehooves and leapt across a pipe manifold and, not missing a beat, Naphtha leapt after her.

Taurus lined up some sample bottles in a carrier and wedged them behind the wheel well. I figured we were going to pull samples from the jet-fuel tank, but he turned past the security shack and made a left toward town. Once again we went down a road with some rickety houses that listed in the shadow of the catalytic cracker, and again the women straggled out toward the truck and retreated when they saw me. Taurus idled the motor and lowered his window. "Sharon, it's me."

A woman in embroidered jeans came up alongside him, her hands jammed in her back pockets. "Scott. You're here early. Who's your little friend?"

Taurus looked as if he were surprised to find me in the passenger seat. "Oh, her. Just someone I work with."

"Good for you." I wasn't sure if she was talking to Taurus or to me.

"You been having trouble with the tap water?"

"When don't we?" Sharon asked, raking her hair from her face.

"I mean more than usual. Any discoloration? Funny taste?"

"You know, now that you mention it, the coffee's been a little funky. Ebony!"

A child approached and pressed her nose against Sharon's thigh. She was holding a nude headless Barbie.

"Ebony, did you tell me Mrs. Kolinka said something about not drinking the water over there at the school?"

She nodded, still with her face against her mother's jeans.

"Did you call the hotline?" Taurus asked.

"And leave another message?"

Taurus scratched his nose with his thumb. "I hear you, I hear you. Mind if I get a sample?"

"Suit yourself."

Taurus left me alone in the truck with the engine running as he and Sharon went into the house. The girl stayed and watched me. She put her lips around the open neck of her doll and blew into it, not taking her eyes off me.

Taurus trotted down the porch steps a few seconds later, holding in front of him a full sample, gingerly, the way he'd hold a urine test. "Smell." He stuck the bottle's mouth beneath my nose.

I sniffed. "Sulfur."

"Venezuelan Sour." He punched a cork in it. "Only one place that could have come from."

When we returned with sandwiches, Kreigel was up and about with excitement. He had a "get." A predator had taken the bait and was corresponding with Heidi. Kreigel even said "Heidi"—that's how happy he was. "You want to take a look?"

"Not especially," Taurus said.

"Come on, Little Bit. I'll give you a front-row seat." He pushed his chair at me.

Clark was at his own computer, his visor tugged down, and I swear he was laughing. The bosses had all gone to a meeting, and we once again could hear Clark's country Top 40 station.

Kreigel sat in the chair and pulled himself so close to the screen his nose crackled. "Cousteau: Tell me how old you are," he read.

"Cousteau?" I asked.

"He's a French fellow. You know."

"Maybe he just likes diving," Taurus said.

"So I wrote, eleven," Kreigel continued. "Cousteau: You sound perfect. Do you like big men?"

"Ugh, he's fat," I said. "Fat *and* a pervert."

"No, no," Kreigel said. "Not fat. *Big.*"

Taurus laughed. "You're defending him."

Clark tapped at his keyboard. "It's a relationship," he muttered.

"I'm not defending him. Just don't want to scare him off. We're at the most delicate part of the process."

"Everybody needs a hobby," Clark said.

Taurus twisted a sample tag around the bottle of tap water and left it at the corner for the lab men. Then we went to dig up more glass.

Before relief time Clark summoned me into the control room. When he did that, it meant I was in trouble—I'd forgotten to top off a diesel tank or lube up the centrifugal pumps—and I rattled with dread and anticipation. But Clark didn't scold me. Instead he gestured to his desk and picked up each item: the logbook, the pencils, the Maalox, his coffee cup, and even the little gum eraser he kept in the top left corner. Around each he had scribed an ink outline on the blotter so it looked like a crime scene. "See this?" he asked. "This? This over here?"

"Yes."

"You see where everything goes, right? You see that it was all here. You see this, Amelia?"

My neck tingled. I had only heard him use my real name once before; it was after I overloaded a propylene tank car, and he was so angry I thought my cartilage would melt.

"I need you to see this. In case someone says these things were never here."

"Why would someone say that?"

"Stranger things have happened, Little Shit. Stranger things have happened."

We rotated back on the evening shift. One month since we reported the leak and the bosses still hadn't brought any backhoes or engineers to take a look at it. An EPA inspector with a visitor's badge clipped to his breast pocket stopped by before having break-fast with the QC guys at the Wilmington Denny's. Kreigel was sleepless from keeping his "get" on the line.

"At what point do you call the cops?" Taurus asked.

"Could be any day, Scott. Could be any day. You don't want this case thrown out on the grounds of entrapment."

"Entrapment," Taurus scoffed. "Woe to him who would suggest such a thing."

Taurus was researching our medicine bottles. Successive waves of freed blacks, Swedenborgs, and Moravians had farmed this patch before the company cleared them out in 1910. All that was left of them was their garbage. "This leak must have sunk pretty deep to excavate this motherlode," Taurus said. He called the lab to follow up on the tap water sample, and they told him it was lost.

When we went for our evening rounds, Naphtha did not rise to join us. He was lying in his usual spot, next to his water bowl out-side the pump house door, with a paw thrown in front of his eyes to shield himself from the light. When we came back, he was in the same spot. We knelt beside him. Taurus shook off his neoprene glove and ran his fingers over the dog's ribs. "Hey boy, hey good boy," he said.

Clark found a collapsed Diebold carton in the stockroom that was about the right size. He propped it open and taped down the flaps to make a crate for Naphtha, and then he put him in the back of his truck to take his body home. Taurus asked me to stop for a drink after work, which was the custom when a co-worker died on shift, and he said Naphtha was as loyal as any and brighter than most. So we met in the parking lot at relief time.

"Clark coming?" I asked.

"Clark don't stop."

I figured since he was into jazz and California, Taurus might take me someplace swanky, but we ended up in his truck drinking beer and watching the river traffic in the night.

"We won't be around long," he said.

"Life is short," I agreed.

"That's not what I mean." He took a swig. We were listening to a song that pried open my chest like a rib spreader.

"What is this?"

"Billie Holiday. Listen, I think you and me should run off together before the shit hits the fan. Go to Rhode Island."

"Rhode Island?"

"You want to go to California? I'll take you. I mean, we get along. We already know that from working together, and getting along's the hardest part."

I watched the lights of the dredger float upstream toward the Platt Bridge. I didn't want to run off with Taurus, but I wouldn't have minded spending the rest of my life sitting in his truck, tossing back beers and listening to music.

"You wait for Clark, you wait forever. He's a family man."

I propped my foot on the dashboard. "*You're* a family man."

"Nominally, nominally."

Taurus called his wife the ball and chain, even though at one time she must have had a light touch and activities she enjoyed. A year with Taurus, and I'd be the ball and chain too.

"Okay," he said, turning the ignition. "Don't go with me. But I recommend you go. Soon, and as far as possible. Or if you stick around here, cover your ass."

He did not come to work the next day. I did rounds by myself, without Taurus or Naphtha. It was no fun describing the leak. When I went to the control room to give Clark my readings, the place was silent: no country music, no shift bosses. Even Kreigel was not at his usual place by the computer. Just Clark at his desk and something missing. His hat, maybe; but no, his hat was on his head. Then I realized it was his desk setup: the log, pencils, coffee cup, and Maalox had disappeared. The blotter, on which Clark had carefully traced the tools of his trade—that was gone too.

"That's a fine howdy-do," Clark said, nodding at his blank desk.

"Where's your stuff?"

"I can only speculate."

I pulled a chair up next to him. "I sat in Taurus's truck last night and drank beer with him," I blurted. I'd never said anything personal to Clark before, but I thought my whereabouts might be relevant, somehow.

"Well." He looked at where his Maalox used to be. "You're not the first woman to do so."

That made me feel cheap, like I disappointed him. "He asked me to run off with him."

I studied Clark's face for a reaction, but it just seemed to recede deeper into the shade of his ball cap.

"I guess he was kidding," I added.

"Probably not. You're going to see some unusual things happen here, Little Shit."

"He told me to cover my ass."

Clark's chin dipped to his chest, and when he lifted it, he said, "I think that's a good idea." He did not ask me to run off to Rhode Island with him.

Security came at lunch. These were contracted guys, minimum wage, black guys out of Chester. It wasn't their fault. They took me in one truck and Clark in the other—two of them in the front and me in the backseat. As we drove, I listened to a pop song on the radio, and about the third time the girl singer said, "You saved me," I understood it wasn't pop at all, but Christian music disguised as pop, and it depressed me. We rolled through the distillation units, and everything was running normally; operators and mechanics went about their business. When we encountered another security truck, the drivers stopped to chat through their open windows. Clark would reach the front office before me.

I didn't see him. The security guards took me to a receptionist on the second floor who wore a charm bracelet. She asked if I wanted coffee or water and delivered me to a windowless conference room. I sat at an oval table. At one end of the room a screen was stretched open on a tripod, all set for a training video. Muzak came in through the air-conditioning vents, and on the wall hung a poster with a purplish photograph of a man and a woman holding hands and nuzzling on a beach. Underneath, in a script font: "Productivity." I stared at it a long time before I realized the picture did not match the word.

After a few minutes, five men entered the room. They were jovial, and one called out for a pitcher of water. The young woman smiled at me as she brought it in and poured us water, and I smiled back. I knew one of the men, our unit supervisor, and one was my union rep, and two others I had seen on occasion walking the manifold with their hard hats cocked back on their heads and their neckties flapping in the breeze. One was new to me, and it was clear from where he sat and how the others leaned toward him that he was the biggest boss in the room. He set a loose-leaf binder on the desk and turned the pages slowly. Finally he said, "Amelia, is it?"

My voice spurted like rusty water. "They call me Little Shit."

Good-natured laughter among them. Then he continued: "I think we better stick with Amelia. Amelia, we've been over to the tank farm, and it looks like we got ourselves a problem there."

My scalp tingled with relief. Finally they were going to do something about the leak.

"You know your job is first and foremost safety," he said. "Your safety, ours, and the community's. That's our mission."

I nodded.

"We might have avoided some serious trouble if you had kept that in mind."

I cleared my throat. "What?"

Here the union man intervened. "You understand, Les, Amelia's the junior man on the shift. She's just following the example of the others. And from everything I hear, she's a good little worker. Among the women, one of the best."

I briefly flushed with pride before I remembered there were only eleven of us in the refinery. Being one of the best might have placed me at—what—seven?

The chief guy nodded. He had thinning hair and sorrowful eyes. "Everything I've heard confirms that." He turned to me. "There's been some shenanigans here, and you have the opportunity to put things right."

I liked that word; it made me think of Irish dancers. "There's no shenanigans. Clark's been reporting the leak for weeks. It's in the Secret Crude Line."

The chief guy tapped his pen on his lips. He was dismayed. "You understand in a refinery how things get passed down. Rumors. Legends. The fact is there is no Secret Crude Line."

"Yeah, but there is. And a stain like Kazakhstan."

"We need your cooperation," the top boss said. "The company will stand behind our men. And our ladies."

This was supposed to be a joke, but I didn't laugh. I stared at the phony grain of the conference table and thought how much it resembled eddies of gasoline.

"What does Clark say?" I asked. I didn't have to look up to know they were exchanging glances.

"Let Clark worry about Clark, and Amelia worry about Amelia," the union man said. And it was at that moment I knew Clark was in another conference room just like the one I was in, with five guys who looked a lot like these guys.

"It's tough for women out in the field," the head boss said. "And the company is one hundred percent behind diversity."

General concurrence and throat-clearing.

"We know that sometimes a pat on the back is not just a pat on the back. Sometimes it's unwelcome. If *you* don't want it, it's unwelcome."

My brain was spinning. "Are we still talking about the leak?"

"As I said, *your* safety is *our* mission." He smiled at me very sadly, and I wanted to tell him it was all right, whatever was troubling him. "Has Mr. Clark ever acted in an untoward manner?"

"Untoward?"

The union man clarified: "Has he ever put the moves on you."

Clark? Sure. He had grabbed my shoulders out in the field and pinned me against the tank, flattened himself against me, his hard hat and mine knocking like a couple of turtles in heat. Except this had only happened in my imagination. In real life, once my fingers brushed against his as I handed him an inventory, and that was enough to make his ears turn red.

"It's important we establish a pattern."

"A pattern of what?"

"She's gonna see it on the six o'clock news anyway," the union man said. "Clark's down at the sheriff's."

"It seems," the big boss said, clearing his throat, "he has been looking for young girls on the Internet."

I burst out laughing. "No. That's Pocket! Kreigel does that."

He nodded, the way he'd nod at a stutterer to get her to hurry up. "It was Mr. Kreigel who uncovered this."

"Ironic, isn't it?" one of the other suits said. "Not four feet apart and these two were sending each other dirty messages."

"No, no way." I was still laughing. "Look, if he did—you know. It's what they call breaking stones. Clark was just trying to keep Kreigel busy so he'd stay the hell out of the field."

As soon as I said that, the five of them rolled their chairs to the table and jotted something on their clipboards.

"But I don't know that he *did* anything. No," I decided. "That's not his style. He's not a prankster, Clark." I was about to add, "Not like Taurus," but decided to shut up.

"He did have motivation, though. This is what you're saying?"

"As a joke." The blood drained from my head, and the space in front of me cracked into fractals. "*No.* I mean, there's no motivation."

The man sitting closest to me put his hand on mine. "This isn't evidence. Just corroboration. The sheriff will find all the evidence he needs at Clark's house."

So they found a way to his house. And I knew exactly what they would find—I'd pictured it many times. A spotless kitchen with Formica countertops; a portable CD player and Clark's Kenny Chesney and Tim McGraw discs; a refrigerator full of Ball Park Franks and one-liter bottles of Dr Pepper; his daughters, in the upstairs bathroom, applying lip gloss and arguing over a blouse. Naphtha in the meat freezer. Copies of the pages of Clark's log.

The previous summer, on a day that buzzed with cicadas, Naphtha brought home a lady friend, a spaniel mix. It was his happiest time. He squired her around the tank farm, up to the Casinghead Manifold, and over to the xylene tanks, and he showed her how to bark at the Old Shipping Header and how to skitter up and down the fire banks without losing her footing. Kreigel—this was before he got involved with police work—said in a Bogart voice, "Stick with me, sweetheart, and I'll show you the town." This cracked us up, partly because it was pretty funny, and partly because we'd never heard Kreigel tell a joke before. After that, every time a mechanic or lab man walked into the pump house, Kreigel had to repeat the line, and after a day or so when the spaniel mix disappeared, he'd have to recreate the whole scene—the lady friend, the jaunts around the tank farm, etc.—just so he could get to the punchline, and we quit laughing and Clark had to put on his hard hat and go outside whenever he heard Kreigel winding up.

After the meeting the same security guards rode me back to the pump house, and the first thing I did was gather up the bottles we had found at the leak. By now Taurus was somewhere on the New Jersey Turnpike, close to New York, with the windows cranked down and the hot mists rolling off the Jersey refineries. I hope he picked up good jazz stations clear up to Newport, and that they were playing Dave Brubeck, his favorite, and any thoughts of country-shaped stains and dead dogs and little girls with headless dolls flew out the back of his truck. I took the bottles to my house and lined them up at my kitchen window: green, rose, amber. Blue. Those men were here, and now they're gone.